Wildfire

This Large Print Book carries the
Seal of Approval of N.A.V.H.

Wildfire

Kelly Adams

Thorndike Press • Thorndike, Maine

Published in 2001 by arrangement with Maureen Moran Agency.

Thorndike Press Large Print Romance Series.

The tree indicium is a trademark of Thorndike Press.

The text of this Large Print edition is unabridged.
Other aspects of the book may vary from the original edition.

Set in 16 pt. Plantin by Christina S. Huff.

Printed in the United States on permanent paper.

Library of Congress Cataloging-in-Publication Data

Adams, Kelly.
    Wildfire / Kelly Adams.
       p. cm.
    ISBN 0-7862-3347-8 (lg. print : hc : alk. paper)
    1. Women park rangers — Fiction. 2. Forest fires —
Fiction. 3. Naturalists — Fiction. 4. Large type books.
    I. Title.
    PS3551.D3756 W55 2001
    813'.54—dc21   2001023534

Wildfire

Chapter 1

When she was a little girl, Molly Carter had loved to pretend she was an elf, so small and swift that she could move unnoticed among mortals. That feeling of magical possibility had persisted into adulthood, and today especially she felt its keen presence in the air.

"Fall is full of possibilities," she announced whimsically to the forest around her.

A soft, scolding *chirr* above her head caught Molly's attention, and she looked up to find a gray squirrel lecturing her from his perch. Molly's lips quirked in amusement, and slowly she pulled the ear of corn from her pocket. "You won't feel like arguing when you see what I've brought, chum," she murmured, carefully setting the corn on a nearby tree stump. The squirrel froze, its eyes jet-black beads of concentration.

Molly inched back on the slick carpet of pine needles and took up a position behind a hemlock, resting her hand on the rough bark. After a moment's vigilance, the squirrel started headfirst down the elm tree, stopping occasionally to scout the forest. He paused at the ground for one split second, and then all pretense of caution disappeared as he eyed the corn greedily. Molly had trekked through this part of the forest several times in the last month, and each time she had brought some corn for the squirrels. Their eager consumption of the food amused her, and she smiled as she watched this one hold the ear with its front paws while it gnawed at the kernels.

A blue jay screamed nearby, and Molly glanced at her watch. It was almost three in the afternoon. She stared up at the canopy of tree branches, which filtered the softest gauze of sunlight onto the forest floor. Reluctantly she picked up her spray gun and moved on. Molly was the forest ranger in charge of timber management in this part of North Carolina's Great Smoky Mountains, and she and her assistant, Gil, had just completed a timber survey. Now Molly was marking the trees that would be sold to a lumber company. Gil was in another part of the forest, checking for diseased trees.

She felt almost primitive as she walked silently through the woods, stepping over roots, ferns, and small brush. There was a clearing to the right, and she stopped to spray a tree on her map, shooting one thin line of paint near the bottom, another four feet up the trunk. She walked to the break in the trees and stood on the overhang of rock. All around her were wild rhododendrons, their last blossoms long spent in the throes of September. Glossy green leaves brushed her cheek as she moved to the edge. Here she was surrounded by mountains thick with trees. The "smoke" of the Great Smokies hung low, drifting like silk pods hung on a breeze. And even though Molly knew the ghostly effect was caused by humidity and hydrocarbons produced by the luxuriant vegetation, she found the sight no less enchanting.

Molly absently brushed some dried leaves from her uniform as she stared at the beauty around her. She never grew tired of it. There was magic here; and when the smoke hung low, there was an air of expectancy, as though some noble savage might step through the trees at any moment. She'd said something like that to Gil one day, and he'd laughed at her fanciful imagination. "You think Henry David Thoreau is going to walk out of the Smokies like he was stepping out of Walden Pond, Molly," he said, shaking his head. "The only living humans here are timber cutters and hikers. And personally, Molly, I can't really see you with one of those hulks."

Gil's teasing remark had touched a raw nerve like a cauterizing iron. He was right. It definitely wasn't a macho man she wanted, not after Steve.

Let some other woman marry that type, the man with a solidly muscled torso, a clinging flannel shirt with the sleeves rolled up over strong forearms, a pack of cigarettes in the pocket. Let some other woman knit sweaters alone at home while he spent his time racing cars, drinking beer, and hanging around with the boys.

Molly was convinced that such men were always known as "the boys" because their social development had been arrested at the age of four. They'd never cooked a meal for themselves in their lives, and they seemed to think that the floor was the natural repository of all soiled clothing. And in that strange fraternity, communication with women on any emotional level was forbidden. Strong and silent. That was a real man. They probably had clubs and pledges and secret handshakes, Molly mused. Maybe somewhere they had a clubhouse, and engraved over the door were the words *Real men don't even talk about quiche.*

This was all leading to memories of Steve, and she tried to push them back into the recesses of her mind where it was dark and she would not be forced to examine the circumstances of her marriage and subsequent widowhood. *Widow* was such an unattractive word, she thought. It summoned up the image of a thin, lethargic woman, pale and drawn, a black dress hanging like crepe on her wasted frame, a woman whose face would crack if she smiled.

Molly would have none of that. Left alone three years ago at the age of twenty-four, she had disappointed her friends who had expected her to remain in the small North Carolina town where she'd grown up, mourn quietly for a year, and then marry some eligible young farmer or insurance salesman. But Molly had been enchanted by the forest ever since her father had taken her to collect pine cones as a child. She had gone on to study forestry in school, and after Steve's death it had seemed natural to return to the forest, the one place where she felt really at home.

She was well aware that more than a few people considered her peculiar. "Why ever would you want to spend all your time alone like that?" her friend Jennifer had asked just the other week. "I mean, how can you do it?"

Molly wasn't sure whether Jennifer was more dismayed by the fact that she chose to live without a man — or that in many ways she actually lived *like* a man. With her delicate bone structure, long neck, and wide blue eyes, Molly gave the appearance of fragility. Short black hair curled softly around her face, enhancing the illusion. But it *was* an illusion. Molly Carter was not made of glass. To Jennifer, she'd laughingly answered, "Who knows — If I spend enough time in the forest, I might run into a modern-day Thoreau."

Now, even as she moved through the trees, marking the trunks while her thoughts drifted, some warning penetrated Molly's consciousness, bringing her up short. She thought she detected the sharp, acrid smell of smoke and lifted her head sharply, like an animal sensing danger. Raising her binoculars, she searched the forest. She couldn't see any smoke, and already the smell seemed to have faded. She closed her eyes, lowering the binoculars, and concentrated on the faint stirring of a breeze. Slowly she inhaled the pine scent surrounding her.

A twig snapped, and Molly's head jerked around, her eyes searching the dark enveloping leaves of the trees. He stepped out from between two black oaks, and Molly went rigid. He was walking slowly and deliberately toward her, and she noticed a slight

12

stiffness in his gait. Dappled sun caught flecks of white in his chambray pants as he approached, his slim hips moving in a sinuous rhythm of their own. He wore a coarse cotton shirt, dark blue, the long sleeves just brushing the fine bones of his wrists. Long hands, also fine-boned, swung at his sides, one of them gripping a walking stick. His shoulders and neck appeared to be strong but without bulk. Dark brown hair lay neatly and somehow sensuously against that sculptured head, which was as compelling as the head of a magnificent Arabian stallion or a wild lion in the jungle. His lips parted slightly, surprise and interest mingling in a pair of incredibly green eyes flecked with yellow. She was struck by those eyes. They were the verdant green of the forest lit by streaks of sunlight. They were dazzling. And they were staring at her. She stared back and decided they were the eyes of a poet. He must be an apparition, a ghostly presence she'd summoned up with her idle thoughts of Thoreau.

The apparition spoke as it came to a halt before her. "Hello," he said softly, his voice rich with a mellow huskiness that would have been pure gold if voices were metals. "I saw some smoke on the hillside over there. I was going to check it out." Molly turned in

13

the direction he pointed and lifted her binoculars to her eyes. Now she could see a thin wisp curling up from a valley, but the forest blocked her view. It could be a hiker with a campfire or it could be trouble. "I'd better check," she murmured. "My jeep's back here."

"I'll come with you."

He fell into step beside her, his stride long and easy, although she could still detect that stiffness in one leg. She also noticed a thin scar high on his forehead, disappearing into his hair. He must have been in an accident. Her eyes fell to the walking stick, and she made out the letters *S-e-a-n*. Sean. She couldn't quite make out the last name, but it looked like it started with *F.*

"I'm sorry," she said. "I forgot to introduce myself. I'm Molly Carter."

His sideways glance was warm and gentle. "My fault," he said at once. "I was so distracted by that smoke. Nice to meet you, Molly. I'm Sean Feyer."

"Fire?" she repeated incredulously, pronouncing his name as he had.

He nodded ruefully, giving her another sideways smile that seemed both patient and slightly weary. "Spelled *F-e-y-e-r,* pronounced like smoke and fire."

It sounded like a recital, something he'd

14

said many times before.

He climbed into the jeep beside her, and Molly followed the logging road in the direction of the smoke. "Interesting to find you in the Smokies, Sean Feyer," she ventured, pleased when she saw his sunny smile again.

He nodded. "One of those accidents of a name. The plumber called Pipe or the dairyman Farmer." He stared intently off into the distance, and Molly stared at his profile. She judged him to be about thirty. He shifted the backpack he was carrying and said, "I was collecting some rocks and taking nature pictures for the Freestone Foundation. We're putting together an exhibit for children."

Molly's heart glowed with appreciation. She had spoken to the Freestone Foundation once in her capacity as a forest ranger. It was an environmental group, a solid, respected coalition of businessmen and artists banded together to promote conservation. She pictured Sean Feyer seated at the polished mahogany table in the Foundation's board room, surrounded by lawyers, executives, poets, and painters, all united to preserve wilderness areas like this very forest. He had said he was photographing the forest for an exhibit. That must be it — he

15

was a nature photographer. He was obviously the artistic type.

"Are you a photographer?" she ventured, watching his sinewy hands on the walking stick.

"At the moment," he said, a touch of irony entering his voice like a cloud passing over the sun on a bright summer day. "Otherwise I —" He broke off suddenly as they topped the short rise, and sucked in his breath.

Molly followed his gaze and felt her own muscles contract. In the valley below she could see the first flames like dragon's breath as they danced on the pine-needle carpet of the forest floor. They hadn't spread upward to the dry, brittle treetops, but it was only a matter of time . . .

Suddenly time became very important. Neither she nor Sean spoke of the fire, as though the very mention might cause it to spread. She pulled a radio from her utility belt and called Gil. His usually bantering tone was sober, apparently subdued by the urgency in her voice. She gave him her location and told him to call the fire tower and notify the firefighters immediately.

Now it was up to Molly to do whatever she could until help arrived. She grabbed a shovel and a fire extinguisher from the jeep and sprinted toward the fire, only vaguely aware of Sean's loping presence behind her. He followed her unhesitatingly toward the flames, Molly noted abstractedly, her mind already estimating the wind velocity and the size of the fire.

The blaze consumed dry grasses, needles, and brush in a line about twenty feet wide, and Molly headed straight for a pine tree where flame licked up the bark like a fawning dog. She aimed the fire extinguisher at the base of the tree and kept spraying until she was sure the danger there was past. Beside her, Sean had removed his shirt and was beating down a small blaze near another tree. She turned to help him, and he moved back as she once more made use of the extinguisher. But no sooner had they put out those renegade flames than several others sprang up. There were too many for the two of them, and an instant later they heard a rifle-crack explosion as fire leaped up a pine tree and devoured the dry top. The wind had increased, and now the flames in the tree stretched toward other trees, greedy and wild.

Molly swore softly under her breath. The blaze was too far gone now for the two of them to stop it. They'd have to move to a safer distance until the firefighters arrived with the hose. And then it was too late even for that, as the fire suddenly launched itself overhead from one treetop to another and raced down the trunk. In the blink of an eye, the forest floor became a bed of flames, rolling and broiling and crackling. The noise was horrendous, the sound of living forest dying in an instant. No matter how many fires Molly battled, she would never stop fearing and hating that sound.

She and Sean moved closer together, both turning to assess the ring of flame that surrounded them, drawing ever closer.

"A trench," Molly shouted above the deafening roar, and he nodded. She aimed the fire extinguisher at the ground and sprayed a large circle. Sean had taken her shovel and now he began digging quickly and efficiently, his face grim. Despite the dry weather, the earth was loamy, and Molly knelt to scoop out soil with her hands. When the trench was big enough, Sean threw down the shovel and took her hand. He helped her into the trench and she lay right down on the damp ground. Sean climbed in beside her, and they both began raking loose dirt over themselves.

Sean pulled Molly close to him, his arm encircling her protectively. He pressed her head against his shoulder, and her mouth touched his neck. Above them she could hear the uncontrolled devastation of the fire, like an angry giant on a rampage. Here in their burrow, like two animals, Molly could feel his regular heartbeat and the tightness of his muscles. The musky smell of earth filled her nostrils, mingling with the salty scent of his warm, moist skin. She knew that above them the flames were feeding like insatiable, monstrous babies, sucking the life from the trees, boiling their sap, turning their limbs and leaves to ashes.

Here in this cool, dark tunnel, Molly was undergoing a transformation of her own. Her skin prickled as the long length of Sean's legs pressed against hers, his bare chest touched her cheek, and the even cadence of his breath brushed her hair. All this called up a fire of a different sort — flames that began deep inside and worked their way out to the flesh, scorching her where she had thought herself untouchable. Her breath came harder.

It was impossible to move away from his touch, so she lay still, feeling her own heartbeat accelerate with each slight movement he made, feeling her breath grow more uneven.

The roar above them became dimmer. And then his voice was like a rumbling breeze against her ear as he said, "It's safe now. The fire's passed."

But neither moved.

In the dark like this, so closely pressed against his strong male body, Molly was forced into a vivid awareness of Sean and, in turn, a vivid awareness of herself. His muscles were hard yet yielding against her softness.

Alone in the forest for long periods of time, she had grown accustomed to ignoring her own physical presence, attuning herself instead to the surrounding trees and wildlife. But now she was acutely reminded of her own femininity, of the softness and shape of her breasts and hips as they touched Sean's body. Strange. She had no sense of embarrassment, only a kindling that felt like gnawing hunger.

The crackle of a radio broke the spell holding them in their earthen cocoon, and both stirred at the same time, kicking away their blanket of dirt as they sat up. Sean climbed out first and reached down to help Molly. His hand clasping her own was as intimate as their embrace in the trench, and Molly shivered slightly as the cool flames of awareness flickered throughout her nerve endings. Tentatively she met his eyes, as dark and inviting as the depths of the forest.

"You okay?" Gil called as he picked his

way toward them through charred under-brush, still-smoldering tree trunks, and fallen branches. Molly offered a lopsided smile when she saw the concern on his freckled face. Red hair refused to be confined under his hard hat and escaped in ludicrous curls. His red-yellow eyebrows ran rampant above round, owlish hazel eyes.

Molly nodded. "We got caught between two fire lines and had to dig a trench."

There was no time for introductions. The faint throb of the approaching helicopter reached them, and Molly instinctively took charge. Twenty men in fire gear came running through the forest, and she lined them up to work the hose that the helicopter fed to the ground.

She moved back and forth quickly and efficiently, positioning the men in strategic areas in relation to the fire line, ordering the digging of trenches, directing the spray of water. Carrying her own ax, she worked her way through the underbrush, felling small trees, and creating a fire barrier.

She moved up the length of hose at one point, shouting over the din of crashing trees, pounding water, and sizzling flames. She wanted Gil to direct the spray more to the left, where the fire was threatening to skim along the top of the pines again. She held her radio to her ear, while the helicopter pilot reported on the direction of the flames from the air. As she turned around, she found herself staring straight into the bare chest of Sean Feyer. Her eyes moved slowly up to his face. It was stained with soot and dirt, as she knew her own was, but the riveting stare of those emerald eyes brought her heart to a thudding crescendo. He reached out and gently brushed a twig from her hair, his hand lingering there. A thin ripple of pleasure ran through her. His touch felt so blatantly sensuous that she licked her lips unconsciously.

"Gil saw some small animals running for shelter," Sean said, his hand slowly lowering. "I thought I might take my camera and try to get some pictures."

Molly considered briefly. "They're headed for a stream over there," she said, her eyes moving in that direction. They'll be all right if they make it. I don't want you risking your safety."

He regarded her a moment longer without speaking, then nodded and went back to the fire hose.

Molly trotted off to the left, speaking into her radio as she went. She'd never yet hesitated to give a man an order, but somehow she had the impression that nothing anyone said to Sean Feyer would stop him from doing exactly as he pleased. She glanced back over her shoulder and saw that he was no longer manning the hose. Her eyes narrowed as she scanned the area, but she saw no sign of him. Damn. He was a civilian, and she was responsible for his safety.

Right now, however, she had a forest fire on her hands, and she couldn't abandon her position of responsibility to go searching for Sean. He was on his own.

The sun had long since set by the time Molly and her men killed the fire, and she was exhausted. The chill night air lent an eerie haunted aura to the scene. For acres in every direction the ground was strewn with steaming rubble, charred and misshapen. Trees once capped with lush green foliage now stood denuded like stark, dead monoliths. *Dead.* That was what fire did to a forest — turned it into a graveyard. She hated the waste and the carelessness that sometimes caused it. The whole scene left a bitter, acrid taste in her mouth.

The relief crew came jouncing up the mountain in jeeps, their headlights piercing the smoky dusk like ships on a foggy sea. Molly leaned on her shovel as the weary, grime-streaked men began climbing into their own jeeps. It was time to go home and get some rest. The relief crew would stay on the mountain until morning, tamping out the last smoldering remnants of the blaze. Molly and her crew had won out over the fire this time, but her taste of victory was incomplete. Although the conflagration hadn't claimed the whole forest, it had snatched — and destroyed — a portion of it. In every battle the victor lost something precious, Molly thought. This time it was fifty acres of wilderness forest.

Molly stirred when her eye caught a movement at the edge of the charred stand of trees before her. Sean stepped out of the blackness and into the twilight, walking slowly, a shovel in his hand. Molly's lips tightened in rebuke when she saw him.

"What do you mean by going off like that?" she demanded sharply, planting her feet and crossing her arms. "You were my responsibility, and if something had happened to you I would have been in trouble."

"I'm glad to hear I'm in such capable hands," he murmured with a wry smile as he approached her, and Molly felt the blood rush to her head, leaving her slightly dizzy. That musky voice and those lush eyes did strange things to her. Or maybe she was just weak with weariness.

Sean stopped in front of her, a crooked

smile lending an air of dreaminess to his eyes. There was a soft sound from the vicinity of his arms, and Molly glanced down to see a tiny raccoon nestled there. Much of its hair had been singed off, making the creature seem incredibly forlorn and vulnerable.

She ran a practiced eye over the animal and decided it was lucky to have survived the fire at all. One hind leg appeared to be severely burned. No doubt the raccoon would have limited mobility for a while.

"I found him alone at the base of a tree," Sean said. "The rest of his family must have died in the fire."

Her anger at Sean faded as quickly as it had flared. The sight of him standing there with a baby raccoon cradled in his arms brought back the image of the gentle poet, turning her spine to mush. "Come on, you poor thing," she cooed to the raccoon. "Let's get you fixed up."

Sean climbed into Molly's jeep and pulled a light blue sweater from his knapsack while she gave final instructions to the new crew. She studied him as she walked back to her jeep. He looked as tired as she felt, and as dirty. Was it her imagination, or was he watching her approach with the same gentle, protective gaze she'd seen him give the raccoon? The speculation warmed her in the chilly night, and she smiled the bemused smile of a woman in a daydream. Sean Feyer. He had walked out of the forest and into her life in a most unreal way.

She drove in silence back to the ranger station, feeling a kinship with the man who sat beside her, so perfectly still and peaceful, a kinship that was unspoken but of blood-bonding depth. She wanted to know him, everything about him, but she was sure she knew everything already. There was no artifice to him. His simplicity and gentleness were clearly written in his every glance and gesture.

At the station he got out of the jeep slowly, careful not to disturb the raccoon. He carried his walking stick and knapsack in his free hand.

Molly pushed open the door to the log house, standing in the shelter of the shake-shingled porch a moment to savor the stillness of the night.

She led Sean to an inner office, which housed a desk, filing cabinet, bookcases, and supply closet. This was the station's most businesslike room. She examined the raccoon while it rested in his arms, its black eyes curious but calm. As she'd originally suspected, most of the damage was to its right hind leg and the top of its head. She ran a warm bath in the sink and together they lowered the raccoon into it. The wounded creature protested with a hiss of pitiful bravado. But it soon settled down as Molly gently bathed it. Sean got a clean towel from the drawer she indicated, and she placed the wet animal in his arms again, watching with an amused smile as he awkwardly dried it off. The golden hue of his chest and the black matted hair revealed by the deep V neck of his sweater summoned such vivid memories of his embrace in the dark trench that she nearly groaned. "You'd be great with a baby," she said, only half teasing. His glance was both alarmed and bemused. "I may be a passable mother raccoon to this undiscerning fellow, but humanity panics me."

His confession only made her warm to him more. He was shy, and he was uncomfortable around people. She liked that.

Molly prepared a syringe with antibiotic, administered that to the raccoon, and then dressed the burns with antiseptic ointment.

She opened a sack of the dry crunchy feed kept on hand for the local wildlife and offered a handful to the raccoon. He backed farther into Sean's arms and Molly laughed. "Here, Mama," she said. "Feed your baby."

Lifting his eyebrow wryly, Sean took some of the food from her and offered it to the raccoon. The animal sniffed delicately and then greedily began pawing at it.

Watching Sean, Molly couldn't help comparing him to Steve, and she felt a momentary constriction of her heart. The closest Steve had ever come to wild animals was when he took one to the taxidermist to have it mounted for his den. Not that Molly was against hunting. She knew that many of the game animals would die of starvation and overcrowding without it. But Steve had been unable to see an animal as anything more than a quarry to be captured. Grace and cunning and beauty meant nothing to him. He'd had no appreciation of the forest, and had laughed at Molly's training as a ranger. He never said that women should stay at home cooking and cleaning — that was something, she supposed. But she knew he'd wanted her to take a nice nine-to-five job as a secretary somewhere. That way she could add to their income and still be available during the hours Steve chose to be home. Which weren't that many, she thought bitterly.

"What shall we call him?" Sean asked, and Molly looked up in surprise, jarred out of her reverie.

"The raccoon," he said, studying her intently. "I hope you aren't the kind that goes in for names like Ricky Raccoon or Bandit."

Molly grimaced. "I'm totally devoid of sentimentality," she mocked herself. "What do you think of the name *Thoreau?*"

His sudden smile registered surprise. "A good choice. I take it you admire the man."

Molly nodded. "He understood the importance of being your own person. Of living on the land without violating it. And he knew what most men never learn — that material possessions are the heaviest burden of all."

She grew uneasy under Sean's slowly widening smile and amused glance as he leaned back against the sink. Surely she hadn't misjudged him. Surely he wasn't laughing at her.

"I like philosophical passion in a woman," he said with a grin. "Passionate opinions denote a strong personality. I take it your sympathy with Thoreau's views on material possessions had a lot to do with your decision to become a forest ranger."

Molly took a deep breath. The way he'd said "passion" had momentarily robbed her of the ability to speak, and warmth flooded her face as he continued to watch her. "Forests fascinate me," she admitted. "I love the ecology of them and the constant change.

And the solitude," she added, as though categorizing a fault.

"It's unusual to find someone in this day and age who actually enjoys solitude," he said, continuing to level those incredible eyes on her. "Are you a rarity, Molly?" There was a warm glow in his eyes that Molly found more hypnotizing than any physical flame she'd ever seen. The constriction of her throat precluded a serious answer. The words would have emerged choked and far too revealing. Instead, she adopted a bantering tone. "*Oddity* might be a better choice of words," she admitted.

His smile was beguiling and far too enticing, but before the intimate closeness of the small room and the light in Sean Feyer's eyes could ignite the fuselage of her rocketing pulse, Thoreau shifted in his rescuer's arms and yawned.

"Time for bed already?" Sean asked lightly. "Don't you know you're nocturnal?"

"He's probably worn out from all the excitement," Molly said, shifting her attention to the raccoon. "Here, I'll take him." She held open the door of one of several small, wire animal cages that were kept in the ranger station, while Sean set Thoreau inside.

"Your arm," Molly exclaimed, frowning

in concern as she noticed a long cut caked with dry blood on Sean's forearm above his pushed-up sleeve.

He glanced down ruefully. "I got in the way of a falling tree."

"A falling tree! You could have been killed!" Her earlier anger at his failure to obey her orders during the fire flared anew. "What kind of crazy stunt was that, taking off when I told you to stay near the firefighters?"

He wasn't even slightly ruffled by her fury, she thought with growing irritation. He leaned back against the counter and crossed his arms. "I wanted to get some pictures of the fire," he said. "The smoke was too low for a good shot where you were." As if that explained it, she thought, noting the complacent look on his face.

"Pictures aren't our most important concern when there's a forest fire, Sean," she reminded him.

"I'm well aware of the dangers of forest fires," he said, and the ring in his voice carried a conviction she'd seldom encountered. Molly hesitated, and Sean's demeanor immediately changed. He lifted his shoulders contritely, and his voice was cajoling when he spoke again. "You were in charge, and I shouldn't have wandered off," he said. He glanced at her face hopefully. "A moment ago I was anticipating some tender loving care for my arm."

Slowly Molly inhaled and relaxed. He was always a step ahead of her, and that threw her off-balance. She looked at his arm again and decided there was nothing else to do but tend his cut.

He stood quite still under her ministrations. Molly bathed the arm in warm, soapy water, rinsed it, then patted it dry, and finally rubbed on an antiseptic cream. She stared down at his arm, entranced by the sinewy length of muscles, the bronze skin that felt so warm and alive to her touch. She kept remembering the thrill that had run through her when he first stepped out from the forest. She was reluctant to let go of his arm and fussed over it unnecessarily for another two minutes, until she'd nearly exhausted her supply of antiseptic cream.

A strange floating sensation rocked her stomach as she allowed herself to wonder if he'd cut himself anywhere else that she could doctor. Only her ingrained sense of propriety kept her from asking the question out loud.

As Molly began capping the cream, Sean glanced down at his arm, lifted his other sleeve, and then patted his stomach.

"Darn," he said solemnly. "No more injuries."

She felt the blood creeping into her face as she wondered if he could possibly have read her mind. But she wasn't embarrassed, and curiously she took note of the way her eyes remained glued to this handsome stranger even though her brain was ordering them to look at anything in the room but him. Sean Feyer was a naturalist and a photographer, she told herself, and he was gentle and sensitive. He was everything she valued. She suddenly wished she had the nerve to kiss him right there. And yet she almost choked on his next words:

"Well," he said, glancing at his watch, "it's late. Since I hiked up here in the daylight, I obviously can't get back home again tonight. So, Molly Carter, it looks like you have a house guest. Shall I cook breakfast in the morning?"

Chapter 2

Molly woke up to the smell of coffee, and for a moment was disoriented by the aroma. Slowly she remembered Sean. And the provocative images of him that had kept her tossing and turning for much of the night before insinuating their way into her dreams. Her immediate reaction was to close her eyes in delicious memory.

"Are you planning on sleeping all day?"

She peered over the covers, more than a little startled by his invasion of her bedroom. He was standing in the doorway, a cup of coffee in his hand, an intriguing smile on his face. Apparently he'd been carrying a clean change of clothes in his knapsack because today he was dressed in jeans and a soft green bulky-knit sweater that made his eyes look like emeralds. One day's growth of beard shadowed his jaw, and in the morning light he looked more rakish than he had the night before. Her eyes settled on the long curve of his mouth, and her toes curled under the covers as she imagined how his lips would feel on her own. *For Pete's sake, Molly. That's positively decadent. You're barely awake and already you're fantasizing about having Sean Feyer for breakfast.*

"What do you take in this?" he asked, holding up the coffee.

"A shot of whiskey would be nice," she muttered, then managed a weak smile. "Black's fine."

Sean ambled over to the bed and set the coffee on her night table. Rocking back on his hiking boots, he said, "I thought forest rangers got up at the crack of dawn."

"Some of us are less dawn-oriented than others. Personally I'm rather nocturnal."

"You and Thoreau ought to get along fine then. He was up all night exploring the living room."

Sean apparently hadn't slept much better than Molly — though for different reasons. Sleeping on her living-room couch wasn't particularly restful — not with a raccoon for a roommate. Thoreau had immediately climbed back out of the wire cage, having figured out how to manipulate the latch, so Molly had bedded him down in a cardboard box with a towel in the bottom. But the raccoon set up a fuss every time he was left alone, so Sean had moved the box onto the floor beside the couch. When Molly checked on them before going to bed herself, she'd found Sean already asleep on the couch, dark lashes starkly dramatic against his bronze cheek, thick hair boyish and silky on the pillow. His hand was draped over the edge of the couch, and Thoreau was standing on his back legs, his dark eyes bright with mischief as he played with Sean's fingers.

"Where's Thoreau now?" Molly asked, eager to divert Sean's attention, which seemed to be focused on her bare form under the covers.

"When I left him, he was trying to figure out how to get up on the kitchen counter. I suspect he's making pancakes in the blender by now."

"Mmph," Molly muttered, pulling the blanket over her head. Dealing with Sean Feyer and Thoreau at the same time might require more energy than she could marshall at the moment.

"I'm not sure how to translate that, but I'll assume you're awake now. Hurry up and get dressed while Thoreau and I wreck your kitchen."

When she looked out from under the blanket he was gone. She sighed ruefully. The man must be totally lost in his own world not to notice his effect on her. Every time he got within three feet of Molly, her breathing became shallow and labored, her pulse raced off like the beating wings of a startled bird, and she just couldn't seem to stop staring at him.

She drank the coffee while she dressed. From the sounds emanating from the small kitchen she was beginning to think Sean had been serious about wrecking it.

After putting on a clean uniform, she dared a look into the kitchen. Somehow she felt safer around Sean in her uniform, as though it formed a second skin that was more impervious to him than her own. She was greeted by a sight that reminded her in a ludicrous way of a father and his young son trying to fix Mom breakfast on Mother's Day. It was straight out of a Norman Rockwell painting, except that the young son happened to be a somewhat bald raccoon.

Sean was at the stove, humming as he turned fried eggs with a spatula. He was surrounded by a stack of pans, two dirty bowls, a small pile of eggshells, and assorted paper towels, all wadded and stained. Behind Sean, on the opposite counter, sat Thoreau, watching the action while he idly chewed on the flap of a granola-bars box. Molly pried the package away from the raccoon and put it in the cupboard, firmly shutting the door.

"So nice to see two such competent males in the kitchen," she managed.

Sean turned around with a grin. "Shucks, ma'am. Me and my assistant chef were going to bring you breakfast in bed."

"I think I'll pass on the offer," she said primly, keeping her eye on Thoreau, who was stretching toward the cupboard, one paw flailing at the door.

"Breakfast is served," Sean announced, sliding the eggs onto two plates. He took Molly's arm and made an elaborate display of helping her to a chair and holding it out for her. When his fingers brushed her back, she totally forgot the eggs in the heat of longing that rushed through her. Inwardly she groaned. Who could eat while a walking aphrodisiac was serving breakfast?

Her imagination must have been working overtime, even at that ungodly hour of the morning. It seemed that his hands lingered forever at her shoulder blades, thumbs just barely touching the sharp angles of her bones. *More,* she wanted to say out loud. *Another touch.* But it wasn't exactly like asking for another helping of eggs.

She smiled her enthusiastic approval as he set a plateful of eggs, bacon, grits, and toast in front of her, but she was still burning from his touch. Thoreau dropped back to the counter on all fours with a loud thump, and Molly jumped.

"You're not used to having a man around the house, are you?" Sean asked matter-of-factly as he passed her the butter.

"It's been a long time," she allowed, taking pains to spread the butter slowly and evenly, as though that simple act of neatness would somehow compensate for what she considered her messy past.

"A long time since you had breakfast with a man as in casual date, or a man as in husband?"

"I'm not very good at this kind of discussion," she said, her fork making idle circles in the grits. "I was married once, and it didn't work out. His name was Steve."

"Well, I'm glad we gave him a name," Sean said cheerfully, spooning blackberry jam onto his toast. "I take it this is a sore subject with you."

"Just depressing," she said, waving her fork in the air. "By the way, you're a pretty good cook."

"But a bit of a Johnny One Note," he said. "This is the extent of my repertoire. Now if you happen to be dotty over eggs, bacon, and grits you're in luck. I can fix them three times a day."

What I'm afraid I'm dotty over is you, she

thought wryly. What was she going to do if he didn't show any interest in her? The prospect sent a hammer blow to her stomach, and she glanced up at him, stricken.

"What's wrong?" he asked immediately. "You hate eggs and grits?"

She shook her head. How could she tell him that no other man but Steve had ever spent the night with her? She had little experience when it came to fanning the flames of male sexual desire. And now she wondered if Sean felt even a flicker of attraction toward her. He'd given no indication of it. His questions and conversation had been polite but not overly curious.

"I don't suppose you'd like to come with me while I mark trees today," she said, wincing when her offhanded invitation hung on a wistful note.

"I'd be delighted," he said, offering her that beautiful smile again. No man had the right to look so angelic and so roguish with the same curve of lips. It took her breath away, and she hastily swallowed a forkful of grits. He went on, telling her about the rock samples he hoped to collect and the pictures he wanted to take, and Molly chewed and swallowed with no conscious thought of what she was doing. She might as well have been chewing a cardboard box — which, as it turned out, was exactly what Thoreau was doing on the counter. He had found the box of steel-wool pads Molly kept behind the blender and was busily chewing on a corner.

While Sean cleared the dishes, Molly gently pried the box away from the raccoon and got him one of the granola bars from the cupboard. This occupied Thoreau's attention for a few minutes and allowed Molly to turn her own attention back to Sean. From the side of her eyes, she watched him move from table to sink with their dishes. He seemed quite accustomed to kitchen duty as he ran water in the sink and poured in the liquid soap. Morning light streamed through the window in front of the sink, diffuse and cool, and where it touched his dark hair it became suddenly warm, picking up flecks of gold. Even the sun seemed to lavish its attention on Sean Feyer. His face was like fine statuary in the swirling light, and Molly was overwhelmed by a strange keening hunger as her eyes followed the line of his shoulders and arms to the strong hands immersed in the water. She stroked Thoreau absently, her entire field of concentration centered on Sean. She was leaning her elbows on the counter, her face cradled in one hand, her eyes drawn to the soap bubbles clinging to the hairs on Sean's arm. He looked almost magical, those prisms gracing him like fairy baubles. There *was* something magical about him, she thought. She'd sensed it from the moment he'd walked out of the forest yesterday. Maybe it was the poet in him that drew her so strongly.

She laughed softly, and he turned his head, a ready but quizzical smile there for her. "You have a soap bubble on your cheek," she said. "It suits you. You remind me of a poet. You should always be surrounded by poetic images like bubbles."

"Do you really think so?" He brushed at the soap and missed it, and she laughed again. Thoreau had moved closer to the sink and was engaged in the exploration of a large bubble clinging to the porcelain. It popped in his face, and he retreated in hump-backed indignation.

"Serves you right," Molly said, gently scratching the raccoon's neck. She glanced at Sean and saw that he was staring out the window, seemingly lost in thought. He was frowning, and Molly tensed. Sean's mouth tightened, and he raised the back of one hand to rub his right eye before blinking and squinting out the window again.

"Did you get soap in your eye?" she asked hesitantly.

Sean turned abruptly, almost as if he'd

forgotten she was there. "No," he said nonchalantly. "Just a little blurred vision in the right eye."

"From the smoke yesterday?" she asked, immediately concerned.

He shook his head as he drained the water from the sink. "My doctor says it's temporary. Nothing serious." But behind his smile and his light tone she heard something else, and for a second her blood ran cold. Doctor? Temporary? The sudden knowledge that she didn't know Sean at all assailed her and she frowned impatiently. This was the last thing she wanted to hear from her subconscious, and she resolutely shoved the nagging thought from her mind.

Sean didn't seem inclined to discuss his vision problem, and she didn't press it. She was sure he would tell her in time. At the moment it only endeared him to her more. It wasn't just the morning light that rendered him irresistible in her eyes. It was her growing empathy with his vulnerability.

They left Thoreau scolding them in irritation from the newly locked cage — Sean had wedged a stick into the latch to restrain the canny creature — and set out with the paint can in the jeep. Sean had brought his knapsack with his camera and a small pick for collecting rock samples.

Molly followed one of the old logging roads, stopping the jeep where she'd parked it the previous day, before the fire. She paused as she stepped out, staring off to the right and remembering how he'd come through the forest like some splendid animal, all grace and beauty. She turned back to the jeep and found him watching her, the knapsack thrown over his shoulder, his eyes narrowed.

"I was thinking of the fire," she said, immediately impatient with herself for lying. It was the fire within her that was clouding her thoughts.

They walked together through the forest, sidestepping ferns and young pines, stopping occasionally to rest a hand on the rough bark of a hemlock or pine before pushing off again. Sean's presence beside Molly was a palpable reminder of the stirrings inside her, but he seemed so unapproachable, his green eyes dreamily fixed on a small red mushroom or the leaf of a tulip tree.

Birds and squirrels chattered as she stopped at the stand of trees she'd begun marking the day before. Silently Sean wandered a little farther from her. When she glanced back, she saw him inspecting the rocks at an outcropping of granite several yards away.

Following the map made on her timber survey, she moved efficiently through the forest, banding those trees included in the timber contract. Every few feet she stopped and stole a glance over her shoulder at Sean. He was apparently engrossed in the rock, and she watched him hold the camera to his left eye and adjust the focus. That led her back to his vague reference to a vision problem and the underlying vulnerability she'd sensed. Even as she stood staring at him, a part of her was back there beside him, bending down to inspect the rock, brushing his shoulder intimately. *Smitten.* That's what she was. It was an old-fashioned word, a word her grandmother would have used, an appropriate word to be found on one of those cute greeting cards with sad-eyed puppies on the front. But that's what she was — smitten. She was drawn to this man because he was so unlike Steve. He conjured up images of lovers snuggling under a homemade quilt on a winter night or touching mittened hands to each others' cold noses after the first snowfall. Sean was like a drug that entered her body when he held her close in the trench, and now she needed his touch again, couldn't get enough of the sight or feel of him.

And all he had on his mind was a rock.

Molly shook her head and turned resolutely back to the tree.

They stopped for lunch when the sun was directly overhead, turning the forest floor into a mosaic carpet of yellows and greens. Sean led her past the granite rock and through some thick undergrowth to the bank of a mountain stream. "Let's eat here," he said with boyish enthusiasm. "No reservations necessary. Tie and shoes optional."

She had packed a picnic lunch of ham-and-cheese sandwiches and apples. They ate in silence in the shade of a rhododendron, moss-covered rocks at their feet, the stream a gurgling glitter in the sunlight.

"Look," Sean said, drawing Molly to her feet when she was finished eating. He led her to the edge of the stream and hunkered there, pulling her down beside him. "Careful. Don't move." His eyes were intent on the stream, but Molly found her own gaze coming back to rest on his face. "Over there," he said softly, and she forced her hungry gaze away from him and toward the water where he was pointing. She could barely discern the colorless shape, almost a shadow against the rocky streambed, still as a stone. "A crayfish," Molly said, her mouth curving in delight. A leaf drifted down to ripple the surface of the water, and the crayfish danced backward with lightning speed, churning the muddy bottom to a froth. When the water settled again, he was hidden behind a rock.

"There goes a dragonfly," Sean said, pointing once more, and Molly watched the silken-winged insect dip low over the water. "Did you know they can spot a gnat at twenty feet?" Sean said.

"Really?" she murmured, entranced by the way his hair curled slightly over his ears. He was only a foot away. All she need do was reach out, and she would be touching him.

"There's a small waterfall farther downstream," she said suddenly, standing up and looking away from him. She could feel him rise behind her, slowly, and she was sure, curiously. Her swift change in tone had been too abrupt to escape notice.

She started off beside the stream, and a moment later he caught up with her when she stopped to stare out at the waterfall cascading down a smooth rock wall. His hand brushed her shoulder in a gesture of concern. "What's wrong, Molly?" he asked softly. When she only shook her head in denial, he gripped her shoulders with both hands and forcefully turned her to face him. Behind her she could hear the pounding of the falls meeting the stream below, and an answering pounding rose in her breast as she stared into Sean's emerald eyes. His finger reached out slowly and traced a line down her cheek, drawing an answering shiver of pleasure from her. "Are you cold?" he asked solicitously.

She shook her head almost violently. "Sean," she began hesitantly, meeting his eyes, then rapidly dropping her own again. She cleared her throat and tried again. "Sean, how do you feel about me?" Oh, Lord! That sounded like something out of a bad movie. She immediately brought her hand to her obviously feverish forehead, brushing it, then touched her lips with her fingers.

He was regarding her curiously, his gaze thick with some emotion that caused the pounding inside her to grow in intensity. "Molly Carter," he said softly, "may I kiss you?"

Her hand fell away from her lips. "Yes. Yes," she replied in tones first of surprise and then of delight.

His hands left her shoulders and stroked her hair carefully and tenderly. Sean leaned back against the smooth, gray bark of a beech tree and gently pulled her to him. One hand caressed the nape of her neck, his thumb delicately brushing her earlobe.

Tremors ran through her whole body, and the pounding of the waterfall echoed in her ears. His other hand lifted her chin and then trailed softly down her neck, unbuttoning the top button of her uniform. She didn't resist. If he'd pulled her shirt off, she wouldn't have resisted. He spread the collar and then framed her throat with his fingers. Molly was hungry for him, and she strained closer.

His green eyes mirrored the forest and the mountains, and they were as smoky as the distant horizon. Molly had never wanted anything so much as this kiss.

His thumbs were mounting a slow, sensual assault on her throat, where a pulse hammered in near delirium. Every nerve ending in her being charged with electricity. She pressed her palms against his sweater and felt the solid wall of his chest beneath the soft wool. She stood there, paralyzed with desire, as his head lowered to hers, long lashes veiling his eyes at the last moment. Her lips and tongue felt swollen with need, and at the first warm whisper of his breath her mouth parted in welcome. His lips took hers, tentative at first, inciting the shudder of heat that swept through her veins. She was confused. How could this all seem so new to her? She'd been married. She'd thought she knew whatever it was you were supposed to know about making love. But this was beyond any desire she'd known before. His mouth took hers in a way that made her feel he was claiming her body as well. Her legs were pressed against the hard line of his jeans, and her hands wound around his neck, exploring the coarse hair there. His tongue entered her mouth in ruthless pursuit, his hands sliding to her back to push her even tighter against him.

He made two more hungry passes at her mouth, touching and teasing, and then he straightened his head to look at her, his hands resting on her hips.

She slowly lowered her hands, fumbling with the button on her shirt, knowing that his thoroughly devastating kiss had wiped all vestiges of reservation off her face. At the moment, she couldn't even pretend that desire wasn't still raging in her blood like a fever. Her gaze was naked.

"I certainly got what I asked for, didn't I?" she said shakily.

He smiled and reached out to touch her hair. "If I remember correctly, I was the one who asked."

His hand was stroking her dark hair back from her forehead, and that simple action was making it difficult for her to breathe.

"That's the gentlemanly thing to say," she reminded him. "I didn't have the nerve to ask."

He shook his head slowly and drew her to him, laying her head on his chest. She wondered what he thought of her. He'd held her in his arms while a fire raged above them, and he'd spent the night in her home, but it was she who'd had to initiate their first kiss. Why did she have to be the only one smitten in this particular twosome? And what did you call the smitten person anyway — the smittee?

She smiled unwillingly against his chest. Slowly he sank to the ground, pulling her down with him. He sat with his back against the tree and Molly cradled across his lap.

"You know, you didn't have to kiss me out of charity," she offered with plucky aplomb.

"Haven't you ever heard that things are not always what they seem?" he demanded, his green eyes lighting up with amusement, tilting his head to tease a smile from her. He fished in his pocket and pulled out a rock, holding it up to the light. "Do you know how many people over the long years of history have practically killed for a rock like this?" He eyed her speculatively, turning the rock in the sunlight, so that the myriad yellow facets grabbed the sunlight and made it their own.

"Fool's gold," Molly murmured softly.

He nodded. "Pyrite. But it masquerades as something far more valuable and rare." He shoved the rock back into his pocket. "Now tell me about Steve. Was he just pyrite or the true rarity?"

She smiled in spite of herself. It had never occurred to her to compare Steve with fool's gold. "I don't know what he was in the beginning," she said honestly. "But within a year, our marriage was in trouble. Steve got bored easily. I suppose that's natural if you race cars for a living. Marriage can't be very exciting compared to that."

"Do you suppose there was any woman on earth exciting enough for your race-car driver?"

She shrugged. To be brutally frank, marriage to Steve hadn't been all that exciting for her, either. "I guess we would have ended up in the divorce courts if he hadn't killed himself in a motorcycle accident."

"So now you have this aversion to men who fool with machinery."

"They do seem to be a breed apart," she said dryly. "Men who fall in love with cars and motorcycles don't need women," she added, repeating a well-thought-over and much-favored maxim of hers.

"The old sexual-substitutes theme?"

"You could call it that."

Sean leaned his head back against the tree, eyes closed, and Molly studied his expression. She couldn't really divine anything from the set of his mouth. She had assumed that a quiet, sensitive man like Sean wouldn't think much of Steve's roughneck style, either. But maybe Sean actually wished that he was more the macho type. She frowned.

His eyes opened, and he looked out over the water as if searching for something. Molly lay still and watchful on his lap, mentally tracing the line of his jaw. It took all of her self-control not to raise her head and brush his neck with her mouth.

Sean sat up suddenly, his eyes narrowing. One long, graceful finger pointed toward the stream. "Over there on that rock," he said softly. "Look."

Molly turned her head and saw three butterflies hovering over a cluster of two-foot-high magenta beggarweeds that waved gently on their wandlike stems. Two of the butterflies were yellow and the third almost black with shining white and orange spots along the edges of its wings. The yellow butterflies were chasing each other near the water, while the darker one flitted around the beggarweeds.

"Tiger swallowtails," Molly said.

"And the dark one?" Sean prompted.

"Also a tiger," Molly said. "But its coloring is like the pipe-vine swallowtail. Birds won't eat the pipe-vine."

"Exactly." He sounded pleased. "Birds can't always tell the difference between two creatures of similar appearance, so why should people expect to be more observant when it comes to their own species?"

"Something tells me this is a variation on your pyrite-as-opposed-to-true-gold analogy."

Sean smiled. "I have the feeling Steve left a bitter taste in your mouth, like a pipe-vine swallowtail," he said, lacing his hands behind his head. "But I'd hate to see you automatically pass up everyone that resembles him on the outside."

Great. Just what she needed. Advice on men from Sean Feyer when all she wanted was to feel his lips on hers again. "Maybe you should write an advice column," she said dryly. "I know several squirrels and at least one raccoon who would find it fascinating."

A rich bass laugh rumbled from his chest as he reached down to ruffle her hair. "I thought you liked the poet in me. Fickle woman. You're just after my body."

His words were so close to the truth that

her hand flew to the top button of her shirt. But it was because of the poet in him that she found Sean so attractive, she reminded herself.

"Women are probably throwing themselves at your body all the time," she said lightly. "And you, dreamy poet, probably never even notice."

"I haven't had much time for romance," he admitted, his eyes fastening on her mouth.

"Too busy with your photographs and rocks?" she teased.

"That's only a sideline," he said. "Mainly I fly airplanes. Nothing more satisfying than a good flight followed by a few beers with the guys." His voice was mocking, and as his eyes swung away from hers, Molly briefly registered the tightening line of his mouth.

"Ha!" she said in derision. Somehow she couldn't imagine those gentle, sensitive hands at the controls of a plane, or wrapped around a beer can for that matter. He was not the adventurous type. Not like Steve. "I'm sorry, Mr. Macho," she said, "but I don't buy that. I bet you even listen to classical music."

His smile was pained.

"I prefer it that way," she hastened to assure him. "You're different, Sean, and I like that."

He gave her a long, searching look, and then his hands cradled the back of her head and brought her mouth up to his. Once again the kiss began tentatively, but it was filled with expectancy. His lower lip moved against her own, swelling it to sweet ripeness. A honeyed softness spread throughout Molly's limbs, and she found herself arching against him. "Molly," he whispered huskily against her mouth. "Molly, we need to talk."

"Later," she whispered back, the word a ragged gasp as his hand found her thigh and stroked toward the very center of this pleasure rippling through her. She gave herself up to the sensations he was creating, the throbbing in her blood carrying desire to every part of her body. The currents racing through her were like the twanging of a bow. Her arms went around him, her hands greedily touching the muscles of his back and the hard planes of his shoulder blades.

She was pulling his head down to hers when her radio, lying beside the remnants of their lunch, crackled to life.

Molly roused herself slowly and reluctantly. Pulling away from Sean's embrace was like leaving a warm bed on a winter morning — painfully wrenching. "Yes, Gil," she said into the microphone grid. Her voice sounded strangely low and husky, and she cleared her throat.

"I wanted to let you know I finished this section, and now I'm going to check on some pines about half a mile farther north. I'll be there all afternoon."

"All right. I'll be marking trees here."

"Check with you later. By the way, remember the guy who helped us fight the fire yesterday?"

Molly turned to Sean and smiled. How could she forget someone who had just kissed her senses into mush? "Vaguely," she said into the radio.

"I thought he looked familiar," Gil said. "I remembered today. He's Sean Feyer. He's a Forest Service fire pilot. Remember that fire two months ago over in Pisgah Forest? He flew that one and his plane crashed. Heard he was hurt pretty bad at the time. Looks like he's on the mend. He's doing odd jobs for the Service now, temporarily. Quite a guy, huh?"

The radio went silent for a moment, and Molly stared at the mouthpiece as if it were some kind of strange flower she'd just seen for the first time.

"Molly?" Gil's voice came back on the air. "You still there?"

"Yes, sure. Sean Feyer's quite a guy." The

57

words felt thick and strange emerging from her closed throat. "I'll talk to you later."

"Okay."

Slowly she turned to Sean and found him standing behind her, his arms crossed over his chest. Somehow he seemed far more menacing and powerful than he had yesterday. Was this the same man who'd kissed her so tenderly? Who'd rescued a raccoon and talked so knowledgeably about butterflies?

"Molly," he said in a low voice.

The jerky wave of her hand stopped him. "No need to explain," she said shortly. "Mea culpa. You tried to tell me, and I didn't listen."

His eyes flashed. "From the sudden lack of color in your face I'd say you still don't want to listen. I can just imagine what you're thinking: Funny, he doesn't *look* like Steve." One hand pushed through unruly tobacco-colored hair.

The thought had been in her mind, whether she wanted to admit it or not. *No, he doesn't look like Steve. He doesn't act much like him either.* She couldn't get the images out of her mind. Steve's ghost seemed to be standing between her and Sean.

Sean's eyes were raking her features, taking in each nuance of emotion that she knew was flitting across her face. "You want to end this before it goes any further, don't you?" he demanded.

She might as well have a neon sign above her head flashing her thoughts; he was reading her that easily. "There's really nothing to end," she managed to say, injecting her voice with as much reason as she could dredge up from the mire of churning feelings inside. "We've just met. It's no big deal."

"No big deal." He repeated her words with an ironical inflection that made them sound like swear words. His mouth was strained at the edges, though one corner tilted up wryly. He jammed his hands into his pockets and stared up at the treetops a moment before swinging back to her. "Did you ever play that game as a child — Red Light? Where one kid is It and stands in front of a whole line of other kids? And when the guy who's It has his back turned, the others try to sneak up on him?"

Slowly Molly nodded. She'd played it often, in fact.

"And," Sean continued, "if the kid who's It catches anyone moving, the one who's caught has to go back to the starting line? Did you ever start to take a step just as the kid turned around, and you tried to stop, but couldn't? And you wobbled back and forth and finally just couldn't help it — you had to take that step forward or fall down?"

He didn't move, but she felt his presence as though he were just inches away. "We've started to take that step, Molly. We can't stop now. It's too late."

"Sean," she began again, trying to sound both patient and emphatic. "I have a busy life. I don't have time —"

"This isn't a game, Molly," he interrupted sharply. "I don't want any manufactured excuses from you. Be honest if nothing else." Assertiveness, power, assured confidence, they were all there in his voice. When she met those emerald eyes, she wondered how she could ever have thought them smoky. Now they burned clear and bright, and the glitter was dazzling. "I'll put it all on the line for you. No games. I want a piece of your life and as much of you as I can get."

She stood rooted to the spot, as immovable as one of the pine trees. A bolt of lightning couldn't have budged her. She had the dizzying feeling that for the last twenty-four hours she'd been cozying up to a hibernating bear. And he had just awakened.

The stillness of the forest enveloped Molly like a thin cloak, so that each rustle of leaf, flutter of bird, fall of pine cone became unnaturally loud. These were the sounds she lived with every day, and suddenly they seemed intrusive, as though the trees were eavesdropping. And all because of the green-eyed man staring at her with stark challenge on his face.

"Pieces are all I have in my life," she stated flatly. "I'm busy, Sean."

The gold flecks in his eyes burned brighter. "You can spare a few pieces for me." It was a quiet declaration of fact, and she bristled at the confident tone in which he made it.

"The answer is no. I don't think you understand." She ran a hand over her eyes. "It's taken me a long time to pull the pieces together, and I'm not about to beggar them out to anyone. I don't need what you're offering — in fact I can't afford it."

He shifted back on his heels, pine needles crunching beneath his weight. A shaft of light pierced the forest canopy and poured over his head and shoulders like molten gold. Her mind registered certain details with mathematical precision she had learned in college, a precision that enabled her to pinpoint flaws in trees that indicated disease, to differentiate markings on a survey map, and to discern minute signals that could spell trouble. Now she registered something in his stance that subtly threatened her fine-honed sense of self-preservation.

"Molly," he said softly, and she tensed at the undercurrent in his voice. "Remember the swallowtail butterfly. Don't make a snap judgment about the kind of person I am based on appearances. That would be a mistake."

She picked her words carefully. "I'm not judging you so much as I'm judging myself. I'm not ready for any involvement, no matter what it's based on."

"That's not true," he said softly. "You're judging me right this minute. It's there in your eyes, in your voice, in the way you're standing there like some kind of violated statue. You're not even going to give me a chance, are you, lady?"

"You don't strike me as the kind of man who needs more than half a chance to get what he wants," she said, tilting her chin up.

A whispering wind wafted up from the pines, soughing as it touched their faces. It made Molly shiver, as if some fortune-teller had lifted the veil of the future and looked away with a sigh.

Sean shook his head with great deliberateness. "I make my own chances." She sensed a sudden impatience come over him. "Molly, you're evading the issue. I told you

I'm not Steve. Why can't you accept that?"

"You didn't even know Steve," she parried. "I think I'm a better judge than you are."

"One more hour," he said softly, moving closer to her. He stopped a foot away and gently lifted her chin with his finger. "One more hour alone with me, and you'll wonder how you ever saw any resemblance between us." His eyes traveled over her face, fastening with arresting intensity on her mouth.

Over my dead body, Molly vowed. "I'm not interested, Sean," she said flatly.

A slow smile spread out the corners of his mouth, and the gold flecks in his eyes glittered. Belatedly Molly realized that something in her face must have betrayed her turbulent emotions. Damn him anyway for seeing through her hastily erected defenses. Her own body was acquiescing even as her brain said no. She was straining toward him, and much to her dismay she realized that one hand was moving slowly toward his chest, not to push him away but to touch the strength there. She stopped the errant hand in time and forced it to her side, rocking back away from him.

But it was too late. His head was lowering to hers, and she couldn't seem to evade that hypnotic gaze. Her lashes veiled her eyes at the last moment, as his mouth closed over her own, starting a wildfire that raged through her blood. She started to protest, but the words died in her throat even as her lips parted at the gentle urging of his tongue. Sweeping away all of her resistance like a winter wind scattering dried leaves, he took her in his arms and pulled her to him. Somehow her hands found their way to his chest.

He moved his lips over hers, his tongue dipping into her mouth, and the heat built in her body. He was like the mountain smoke rolling in over the mountains. It came quietly and gently but with unstoppable determination. Fighting it was futile.

He raised his mouth slowly, stared down at her face, and whispered, "I'll see you later." Her head was still swimming when she saw that he was walking away.

"No, you won't, Sean," she said with all the conviction she could muster when the imprint of his kiss was still burning on her mouth.

He turned to grin over his shoulder. "Yes, I will, Molly," he called, laughing, never breaking his long stride.

"No." But it came out in a whisper, and it might have been the pines talking. Then he was gone, disappearing into the lush depths of the forest. Straining her eyes, Molly stared in the direction he'd gone, but all she could see was the mountain smoke twisting through the trees. For one crazy second she wondered if she could have dreamed up Sean Feyer. But it had been no ghost that made her flesh tingle with the remembrance of his touch.

The paint sprayer must have gained weight during her lunch with Sean, because it felt like a ball and chain to Molly as she resolutely spent the rest of the afternoon spraying one tree after another. Perspiration broke out in a thin line over her upper lip, and a blue jay's scream became an almost unbearable irritation as he followed her from tree to tree, his raucous censorship like a squeaky gate being opened over and over again. "For Pete's sake, leave me alone," she shouted, flinging a large pine cone skyward. With one last cry, the bird fled, a slash of blue and white against the treetops. Molly set down the paint sprayer and pressed weary fingertips to her forehead as she realized she had just lost her temper, with a stupid bird of all things. It was a long afternoon.

Molly stopped on the ranger station porch at the end of the day to rub the back of her neck as she stared at the red ball of sun hanging over the edge of the mountain. She brought her hands forward on the railing and stared out at the panoply of reds, golds, and yellows speckling the land around the station. Traces of green still lingered like the last breath of summer, but in a couple of weeks the colors would rival the most artistic tapestry. She chided herself for not taking enough time to admire the riches around her. Forestry school had been her entrance to this world, but she'd paid a rather high admission price. Biological sciences and math had dominated her training, and its legacy had been the honing of a sharp, analytical mind. That was fine for the forest where much depended on Molly's observations, but she occasionally caught herself reducing human relationships to cold, scientific terms. It wasn't that she was incapable of feeling. But where her own heart was concerned, she not only looked before she leaped, she practically drew up an emotional cost analysis. Maybe she was being overly cautious as far as Sean Feyer was concerned . . .

She shook her head to clear it and went inside the station. Her better judgment told her that Sean was too risky a prospect. She'd trust her instincts.

She let Thoreau out of his cage and gave

him the run of the station while she fixed her dinner: one pork chop with applesauce and green beans. The raccoon came rushing into the kitchen as Molly sat down to eat, and she suddenly detected the strong aroma of Cachet perfume. Eyeing him suspiciously, Molly set Thoreau on the counter and ran her hand over his fur. Definitely wet. "It's been a great day," she told him sternly as she dried him off with paper towels. "I've already hollered at a bird, and you're next, fella. If that was my new bottle of perfume, you're in big trouble." Thoreau groomed his whiskers, apparently undaunted, as Molly headed for the bedroom, the paper towels still in hand. It wasn't the disaster she'd feared, but Thoreau had obviously run amok on her bureau. The Cachet bottle was lying on its side on her makeup tray, her blusher compact afloat in a pool of perfume. Her lipsticks were scattered about the room, and her neat row of fingernail polishes seemed to have been hit by a storm. "Hurricane Thoreau," she muttered, righting the damage.

She got back to the kitchen in time to catch him eating the applesauce from her plate. Molly made a quick count of ten to check her temper, then got the raccoon an apple from the refrigerator and firmly placed him on the floor. Transferring her pork chop to another plate, she ground her teeth together. "This is all your fault, Sean Feyer," she muttered. "You stick me with an orphaned raccoon while you waltz off scot free. When I see you again I'm going to . . ."

She slapped the plate onto the kitchen table and jabbed at the meat with her fork. The picture that had crossed her mind at the mere thought of seeing Sean again was most unsettling. She kept trying to visualize herself with her hands tightly laced around his throat, squeezing, but the image wouldn't materialize. What she saw instead was herself in Sean's arms. Molly attacked her dinner viciously. Already she knew she was in for another sleepless night.

Chapter 3

It was a long, difficult week, and Molly was more than happy to see it end. She set aside Friday evening as her time to unwind. After dinner she made herself a mug of hot chocolate and carried it to the porch along with the paperback she'd bought last weekend. Bundled in a toasty granny-squares afghan, her cocoa steaming on the table beside her, she settled down into a thickly cushioned wicker chair and propped her feet on the railing in front of her.

She read until even the porch light couldn't hold back the encroaching darkness. Spreading the book face down on her lap, she closed her eyes and curled her arms over her chest beneath the afghan . . .

"You look just like my silver-haired grandmother."

At first she thought she'd fallen asleep and his teasing voice was a dream. She fought to control her pounding pulse before slowly opening her eyes. There Sean stood, hands on hips, one foot propped on the bottom porch step, grinning up at her. His hair was tousled from the wind, and in the twilight his eyes had taken on a dusky hue. Faded blue jeans clung to his hips, and a soft leather jacket outlined his broad shoulders. Molly cocked one eyebrow warily. "How did you get here?" she demanded, looking past him for a car.

"I hiked in from the park entrance. It's a perfect night for a walk. Want to join me?"

Molly ignored his invitation as she lowered her feet to the floor and straightened her back. "You wouldn't want to buy a raccoon, would you?" she asked.

"Thoreau?" Sean stuck his hands in his pockets and smiled cheerfully. "I take it he's already qualified himself as a public nuisance. Where is he now? Chained to his cage?"

Molly shook her head. She stood up, trailing the afghan and clutching her book, and held open the door to the station. Nodding toward the living room, she clutched the afghan around her neck as Sean walked up the steps. He peered inside and then began to chuckle. "You obviously believe in rehabilitating criminals," he said.

Molly followed him inside and watched Thoreau poke his head out of the large

70

hollow stump she'd cut for him two nights ago. She'd moved the makeshift playpen onto a blanket in the living room, and Thoreau had claimed it right away.

"So you've been a troublesome house guest," Sean said to the raccoon, who regarded him with dark unblinking eyes. "I guess that indebts me to your hostess. What should I do to make it up to her, Thoreau, hmm?" He knelt down and held his hand to his ear as though conferring with the raccoon. "Good idea," he said, nodding gravely. "I'll ask." He stood up and faced Molly. "Would you have dinner with me tomorrow night? It was Thoreau's idea."

Molly found her mouth quirking in spite of her resolve. She looked down at Thoreau and said, "Tell your friend I'm busy tomorrow night. I'm the speaker at the annual dinner meeting of the local businesswomen's club."

Sean knelt down again, pretended to listen, then turned to Molly. "He suggests Sunday."

Molly raised one eyebrow, pursed her lips, and regarded Thoreau again. "Tell your friend that I play bridge with my mother on Sundays. And stop encouraging him," she added sternly.

"Well, I'll be seeing her more often

anyway," Sean told Thoreau. "I've signed up to work with the logging crew."

Molly's eyes flew to Sean's face, and her fingers tightened on the afghan when she encountered his measuring look. She composed her face as she looked back at Thoreau, who by now had lost interest in the humans and was curling up inside the hollow log. "Come back here, you coward," she ordered, but no twitching whiskers appeared.

"Looks like you'll have to talk to me yourself," Sean offered quietly as he stood up.

"Well, congratulations, lumberjack," she said, snapping her book closed and tossing it on the couch. "That ought to keep you out of my hair for a while."

The brittle tension inside her increased as his eyes softened and the humor died out of them. "Your hair's only one part of you I intend to explore," he murmured.

Molly stiffened, thinking about Sean on the logging crew and how she'd be seeing him every day. It was the kind of thing Steve would have done — rugged, outdoor work. For Steve, it would have bolstered his male ego. What did that kind of work do for Sean? She stared at his face, trying to find some vestige of reckless bravado there, something that would remind her of Steve. But all she saw was a man with a tender smile that made her heart lurch.

Her gaze wavered and she found her fingers balled into fists around the afghan. "I've got to go," Sean said, a catch in his voice. "But there's something I want you to have." She watched as he reached into his pocket and held out a closed fist to her. Slowly his hand opened, and she reached out to him. He placed something rough and hard in her palm and curled his fingers around hers, closing her hand. His thumb stroked the underside of her wrist, and she felt her blood leap to life in response. She knew he could feel her staccato pulse beneath his thumb, but she didn't withdraw her hand. Slowly Sean released her, half smiling, regret in his eyes. "Good night, Molly."

He was out the door and down the porch with his long strides before she'd even caught her breath. She waited until his footsteps had faded on the gravel road that led down the mountain. Only then did she carefully uncurl her fingers. On the flat of her palm lay the chunk of pyrite Sean had found the day they met. He'd polished it up since then, and each shiny gilt surface caught the light from her small table lamp and sent it back to her in warm yellow flashes reminiscent of the golden flecks in Sean's eyes. She could still picture him in her living room, bending down to greet Thoreau.

Quickly Molly set the pyrite on the oak end table, so quickly that an observer might have thought it had burned her hand. She stared at Thoreau a long moment before her shoulders relaxed.

By Sunday Molly still hadn't moved the pyrite, and each time she crossed the room its gold facets winked and dazzled and seemed to call to her. She told herself that she should put it on the shelf that housed her small rock collection. But the shelf was in her bedroom, and for some reason she was reluctant to carry the pyrite in there. A hundred times she walked past the pyrite and told herself she was being totally irrational, but still it sat on the table.

Sean Feyer was nothing to her. It wasn't he that disturbed her concentration or upset her neatly ordered life, she told herself. It was only an oversight that had made her forget her hot chocolate mug until this morning when she discovered it all marshmallow-gooey and chocolate encrusted on the porch where she'd left it Friday night. It was only weariness that had made her leave the afghan in a crumpled heap on the couch that same night. And of course she couldn't remember what page she'd been reading when Sean interrupted her — that book wasn't at all good anyway. She glanced at Thoreau for confirmation and he stared back at her over the top of the log, eyes sharp, whiskers bristling. Molly shrugged. "All right. So the book is a bestseller and it's being made into a movie. I just lost interest in it."

Grumbling to herself, Molly finished putting two candy dishes on the card table she'd set up in the living room. A small stand-up tray next to the table held napkins and a pitcher of iced tea.

She glanced out the window as a car pulled up the gravel road, a subdued sound in the light rain. It was her mother's mint-condition, ten-year-old Plymouth. Enid Carter was a real stickler when it came to taking care of one's possessions, and as a result she owned beautiful fifteen-year-old suits not to mention her grandmother's linen and crystal. Enid had once worried out loud about the possibility of moths destroying her clothes, and Molly's sister Sue had retorted, "Mother, no moth in its right mind would dare approach your closet except to pay homage." It was true. Besides, there were enough mothballs in the Carter household to deter even the Attila the Hun of moths.

Molly hugged her mother as Enid, resplendent in a relatively new rose-colored pants suit, entered the living room. "Hello, darling," her mother said affectionately. Sue followed, giving Molly a peck on the cheek and a cheerful smile. Her dark hair was the same shade as Molly's, but hung straight to her shoulders. "Here, honey," she said, handing Molly a piece of construction paper with a couple of holes cut in it. "Trevor made this in school. He wants you to have it."

"What is it?" Molly asked dubiously, staring at the bits of dried macaroni glued in circles around the holes.

"A Halloween mask."

"How nice." Molly laughed. "Be sure to thank Trev for me." Carefully she set the mask on the end table next to the pyrite, feeling her heart beat faster as the fool's gold winked in the glow from the lamp. Molly waited at the door while her third and last guest negotiated the steps. Maxie McDermott was a small, rotund man whose general contours suggested a pan of yeast rolls. He also looked a bit like Santa Claus, Molly thought. Four years ago he had been Enid's handyman, but now he was practically crippled by arthritis. Enid refused to put him out to pasture, and Maxie retained the title and salary of handyman. These days he spent most of his time sitting on the bench in the Carter back yard, telling Enid how to weed her flowerbed. But Maxie hadn't always been a handyman. He'd been about to retire from a long career as a college journalism professor when Enid had decided to go back to college, through an outreach program. Maxie had become her mentor, and after she found a job doing public relations for a large bank, Maxie had taken on the largely non-profit job as her gardener. They were extremely close, and Molly suspected that it was only the twenty-five-year difference in their ages that had kept them from being more than just good friends.

Maxie squeezed Molly's arm affectionately and laid his umbrella against the wall. He pulled at his earlobe thoughtfully as he joined Sue and Enid watching Thoreau watch them from his hollow log. "You've hired a butler?" Maxie asked with a twinkle in his eye.

"Actually, he's a walking garbage disposal," Molly said ruefully. "His name's Thoreau. A friend rescued him from a fire."

"Thoreau, huh?" Maxie said, smiling as

he reached down to pat the raccoon's head. Thoreau blinked solemnly.

Enid's smile was teasing. "Given your penchant for Walden Pond, honey, I always figured your firstborn would be named Thoreau, but this little fellow isn't exactly what I had in mind. I'll have to knit four booties for him, plus a cap to cover his bald head."

"You never knitted me a cap," Maxie said with feigned hurt, running his hand over the bald spot on top of his head.

"That's because I find your head so attractive," Enid said.

"Maybe I ought to shave off the rest of my hair then," Maxie rejoined, patting the few silvery tufts that ringed his shiny pate.

"Well, maybe you'd better leave well enough alone," Enid said, her eyes sparkling.

"You'll rue the day you adopted this guy," Sue warned Molly. "Believe me. I speak from experience. This morning the dog threw up on the rug, and then the baby peed on it. Motherhood is no picnic."

"I've heard this song somewhere before," Molly said. "According to you, children should be locked in their rooms until they're old enough to support their long-suffering parents. Right?"

"Something like that," Sue said.

"And this from a woman whose son, my grandson, had offers from five kindergartens," Enid said lightly as she moved to the card table.

"Those were hopscotch scholarships, Mother," Sue retorted. "The boy has great feet but no brains."

They all laughed at that and sat down around the table to play bridge. The Carters were a game-playing family. Sundays almost always found them at the card table or hunched over a crossword puzzle or pondering a Scrabble board. They weren't especially competitive, but their games were certainly spirited.

They were all concentrating on the hand in play when Molly heard a tapping at the door. She went to answer it and found Sean grinning at her from the porch, two cardboard pizza boxes cradled in his hands. Molly stared. He was wearing a sea-green sweater over jeans, and his eyes glowed like emeralds. The droplets of rain in his hair and on his eyelashes did nothing to dull his gleaming aura.

"Who is it, honey?" Enid called

"The delivery boy," Molly called back wryly. "Won't you come in?" she invited Sean through gritted teeth.

He gave her a wicked grin as he stepped inside. "You must be Molly's mother," he said, advancing toward the table like a smiling barracuda, Molly thought.

Enid gave him a warm greeting. "So nice to meet you," she said. "I'm Enid Carter. This is my daughter Sue, and this is our friend Maxie McDermott."

"I'm Sean Feyer," the barracuda said, flashing that predatory smile around the table. To Molly's dismay, everyone smiled back, apparently blissfully unaware of his true nature. "I'll just pop these pizzas in the oven," Sean said, "and bring in some glasses." He tugged a bottle of wine from beneath his arm and set it on the table. "Then you can tell me how you play bridge."

"What a charming young man," Enid said as Sean disappeared into the kitchen.

"He's a trespasser," Molly said, disgruntled. "I told him we were playing bridge today, and he just showed up anyway."

She realized she had spoken sharply when she saw everyone looking at her quizzically. Molly shrugged. "He rescued Thoreau," she added, as if that explained everything.

Sean returned and poured everyone a glass of wine while telling them about the pileated woodpecker he'd seen in the forest on his way up. "I stopped the car and got out to watch," he said. "He was magnificent, a wingspread of almost two feet. He was drumming on a limb just like a rock musician. The racket carried all over the forest." It was obvious to Molly that her guests were hanging on Sean's every word. He pulled up a low-backed folding chair, gave it a dubious glance, then flipped its back toward the table and sat down next to Molly, straddling it. He raised his glass of wine and said, "To Molly." Enid and Sue echoed the toast while Maxie said something that sounded like, "To folly." How appropriate, Molly thought.

Sean took a healthy swallow, then rested his elbows on the table and cradled his chin in his palm. "Okay. How do you play bridge?"

Molly raised her eyes heavenward at the innocence in his voice. Within two minutes he was being besieged with instructions from all sides as they played a mock hand for his benefit.

"Here," Sue said as the last trick was played. "Take my place for a while. I've lost all circulation in my legs." She levered herself from the chair and walked stiff-legged around the room. Sean took her place across from Molly, and Molly's concentration immediately deserted her. She found it impossible to remember how many trump had been played, and every two minutes she had to check the number of tricks she and Sean had won. Enid shook her head as Molly trumped Sean's king. "He's your partner, dear. No need to fight him for tricks."

"Sorry," Molly said, quickly taking another gulp of wine.

Maxie and Enid won that hand, and Molly refused to meet Sean's eyes. There was no way to keep her mind on the game while those green eyes surveyed her from across the table. "Why don't you play for a while?" Molly asked Sue. "I need to do a couple of things anyway."

She retreated to the kitchen and began putting together the mini crab quiches she'd planned to serve as snacks. She could hear bursts of laughter and friendly bickering from the living room. The fact that her family liked Sean sent a dark chord echoing through Molly, and she went to stand in the doorway, pensive. Sean looked up immediately, a look of concern on his face. As Molly saw his probing eyes make a quick assessment of her mood, she knew why this man troubled her so. He was capable of making himself a part of her life with or without her consent. Like a wild grapevine, he could take root against the stoniest wall, and thrive there. All attempts to prune him out would only inspire a fiercer determination on his part. She knew this as surely as if he'd told her he was here to stay.

Molly backed away from the doorway and busied herself getting the pizza and crab quiches out of the oven. Well, she had outlasted persistent men before. She could do it again with Sean.

Pasting a fake smile on her face, she carried the food to the living room.

An hour later, the two pizzas had been reduced to a few paltry crumbs, while most of the quiche sat congealing on Molly's best china serving plate. Sean poured another round of wine to a table of laughing bridge players while Thoreau, perched on his shoulder, methodically scooped his paw into a dish of chocolate-covered peanuts. Sean was regaling everyone with his birdcalls in between remarkably astute play on his part. Molly was impressed — and wary. The man could make himself at home in a den of wolves if he wanted.

"Great afternoon," Maxie pronounced in satisfaction as he slapped down the last card of the last trick. "But we'd better get going. I've got to prune back Enid's peonies tomorrow."

Moments later the trio departed, each

kissing Molly's cheek on the way out. Molly stood in the doorway as her guests loaded themselves into Enid's car. Even when the sound of the tires on the gravel road faded into silence she stood staring out at the forest. The rain had stopped, and a stillness settled over the trees as the smoke drifted dreamily through the mountains.

"You have a nice family," Sean said from behind her, and she could almost feel the warmth from his body through her thin blouse. "You can hear the love when they talk."

"What's your family like?" Molly asked suddenly, surprising herself with the unexpected question.

"The love is there," Sean said. "But my folks aren't very demonstrative. My brother and I grew up in private schools, and we came home to housekeepers. My parents were busy with their own careers. It was prep school for us and then an Ivy League college."

"How sad," Molly said quietly.

She could feel Sean's breath on her hair. "Not really. We knew we were loved. It came in little, basic ways when we were children. A hug at night when my father got home late. My mother skipping the women's club tea to help us build a snowman. And letting us put her best hat on his head." She turned slowly to find him smiling at the memory.

"I didn't have a real home after my father died," she said. Now what made that slip out?

He sobered instantly, his eyes seeking hers, and Molly found herself suddenly lost in their lush depths, her emotions flaring like the gold sparks she saw there. Silence surrounded them, binding them together with tensile strength. Molly sensed that if she didn't break the mood now, the circle of his warmth would envelope her irrevocably. She hesitated imperceptibly. She wanted to touch him, but she knew that would knock down another brick in the wall she'd placed between them. Soon Sean would be able to reach inside and make her care. She knew he was waiting for her to tell him all about her childhood.

She steeled her voice. "The rain's stopped. I'd better put on my jogging clothes before it gets dark."

He didn't step aside, and she had to pass within a fraction of an inch of his solid frame. His very essence seemed to reach out to her, as though he were mentally taking her in his arms. "My jogging things are downstairs," she mumbled quietly, walking faster as she approached the steps in the kitchen.

Out of his sight, Molly took a deep breath and leaned momentarily on the banister. She should have shut the door on him when he came charging up with his pizzas and his wine. The man was trouble, and she'd have none of that.

Trouble of a different sort awaited her in the basement. She'd been promising herself for weeks that she would get Gil to help her patch the crack in the foundation, but she hadn't gotten around to it. Now the basement floor was a river of mud, washed in from the recent storm, and the clean clothes she'd taken from the dryer and left in a wash basket on the floor were scattered across the quagmire in wet, dirty clumps.

"Thoreau, you pea-brained furball!" she wailed as she stormed upstairs. Sean nearly collided with her at the top of the steps, and she brushed past him, muttering under her breath about the dubious parentage and breeding habits of raccoons.

She was still grumbling five minutes later as she plopped down on the couch to tie her running shoes. Her jogging suit was a lost cause, so she'd changed into a pair of jeans and a sweat shirt.

Sean appeared at the living-room door and held up his hands. "I know," he said. "It's all my fault for rescuing him. I should have left the pitiful creature clinging to that tree with his injured paw, his big brown eyes pleading with me in vain." Sean shook his head in mock sorrow. "I should have left him with the fur singed off his little head, left him to face imminent starvation."

"Enough already," Molly growled, throwing a pillow from the couch in his direction. She started for the door, trying to maintain her level of irritation as his laughter rang out behind her. "You can let yourself out," she called back to him.

Molly's feet set up a staccato rhythm on the gravel road, matching the steady drip of raindrops from the pine trees. The thud of her feet became a song in her head with insistent lyrics: *Sean Feyer. Sean Feyer. Sean Feyer.* She tried varying her jogging rhythm, but it did no good. *Sean Feyer.*

The soft wind in the pines brushed Molly's face and became Sean's kiss. The errant raindrops that fell on her shoulders were his fingers, feather-light and tantalizing. She'd drive herself mad if she allowed her thoughts to continue in this vein. Resolutely she tried to think of something else. Sean's words about his childhood popped into her head: *We knew we were loved.*

What a wonderful anchor that must be for a child — to know it was loved. She had felt that when her father was alive. And later, after he died and everything came apart, even though she was very young she'd known in her heart that her mother loved her. But on a practical level, she'd been pretty much on her own for most of her formative years. While other children were being tucked in by a parent each night, read a bedtime story, given a glass of water, and wished "sweet dreams," Molly bedded down with an assortment of relatives and strangers while her mother did her best to pull her life together again. More nights than she cared to remember, Molly had put herself to bed and frequently cried herself to sleep. And by the time Molly's mother could finally afford to reclaim her children and give them a home with her, Molly had been in her teens and too old to be tucked in or read to. It was a loss she still mourned. When she had children of her own, bedtime would be different. *When she had children!* The image of two brown-haired, green-eyed tykes suddenly popped into her head. Foolish woman. She shook her head to clear it and started back for the ranger station. Sean would be gone by now, and she felt a curious reluctance to face the empty house. There was always Thoreau, she thought as she steeled herself.

Hazy twilight was settling over the mountains as Molly slowly mounted the porch steps. She pushed open the door and drew up short. Through the doorway to the kitchen she saw Sean standing in front of her ironing board, holding a pair of her silky pink panties up to the light with a grim look. A strangled sound emitted from her throat, and Sean turned to face her.

"Thoreau really dragged these through the mud, you know," he said matter-of-factly, indicating a pile of her underwear on the ironing board. "I was just sorting out your . . . ah, personal items." Beside the panties was another neat pile of lacy bras. Molly blanched. "I think this pair is my favorite," he said cheerfully, tweaking the tiny bow that normally graced her hip. "Not that I'm a connoisseur. Although I am considering taking more of an interest in these things." He dropped the pink wisp back onto the pile and dusted off his hands. "Well," he said with satisfaction, "I ironed your uniform and put it in your closet, and your sweat suit's on your bed. Everything's been through the wash again and looks reasonably clean. Oh, I mopped the mud downstairs. I'll come back when I have time and patch the crack." He scooped her underthings up from the ironing board, ambled into the living room, and deposited them in her numb arms. "You're low on laundry detergent. See you later." He dropped a chaste kiss on her nose and strolled out the door, whistling with infuriating calm.

Slowly Molly leaned against the door. The man didn't play fair. He just didn't play fair!

Chapter 4

Molly headed the jeep back to the station on Monday evening, allowing herself the luxury of self-satisfaction. The tree marking had gone well, and she was almost finished. She and Gil would be free to devote their full attention to the logging crew next week.

Her sense of triumph was short-lived, however. Spotting the pickup parked in front of the ranger station, she ground her teeth together. The man was relentless. She sat in the jeep considering options. She no longer trusted the worn edges of her control where Sean Feyer was concerned. She considered turning around and finding more work to do in the forest until he got tired of waiting and went home, but that seemed too silly. Shaking her head, Molly dismissed the thought. She never had been one to run away from her problems.

Taking a deep breath, she jumped down from the jeep and ran a hand through her short, dark hair. A steady rhythmic tapping came from behind the station, and she went to investigate.

She found him squatting by the foundation, dressed in jeans and a blue flannel shirt. His leather jacket was lying on the ground beside him. He was holding a chisel to the crack in the foundation and striking it with a hammer.

"They say you can gain entry faster by breaking a window," she greeted him.

He threw her a grin over his shoulder and hunkered back on his heels, lowering the hammer and chisel. "Shucks, you caught me. I'd planned to chisel my way in by night and hide under your bed."

The thought of Sean anywhere near her bed made Molly's blood collect in several sensitive spots. Deliberately ignoring his teasing smile, she said, "Just what are you doing to my wall? Or more accurately, to the U.S. Forest Service's wall?"

"I'm fixing it."

"It looks to me like you're demolishing it."

Slowly he stood up and brushed off his pants. "You have to clean the crack before you can fill it in with patching compound," he explained patiently. "You don't want any ragged edges. It's analogous to cleaning a wound before dressing it."

Molly nodded, trying not to look at those mesmerizing green eyes. She watched as he absently massaged one leg with his hand, and she realized he must be uncomfortable. His leg had been stiff when she first saw him, no doubt a result of the plane crash, and it probably bothered him to work in that squatting position.

"I could start some dinner," she volunteered before her brain realized what her mouth was saying. It was too late to take it back, and she swallowed uneasily as the implications of her offer sank in.

"That would be nice. Thank you." His smile was warm, not teasing, and it thawed something frozen deep inside her. Suddenly she was glad she'd made the invitation.

She had planned to throw together a meatloaf tonight anyway and freeze the leftovers for the weekend. She mixed it up and popped it in the oven, then showered and changed into beige slacks and a black cashmere sweater her mother had given her for Christmas. She ran her fingers through her hair, surveying her reflection critically in the bedroom mirror. Impulsively she picked up her makeup case and brushed some blue eyeshadow up to her brow bone. A feathering of blusher on each cheek and she stood back for another appraisal. Molly frowned. Something was missing. Her looks didn't quite match her mood. Thoughtfully she opened her jewelry case and ran a finger over the contents. She found just what she needed nestled beside her old Girl Scout pin. Gold hoop earrings. She seldom wore them. Sue had once said they made Molly look like a gypsy. Well, tonight she felt like one — a little wild, a little free.

She was mashing the potatoes with the old-fashioned metal ricer when he came inside, and she felt him standing in the doorway, surveying the kitchen before she looked up. She watched carefully, pretending an intense interest in the potatoes while his eyes roved the room as if really seeing it for the first time. As though seeing everything through his gaze, she took in the brightly colored butterfly magnets on the refrigerator, the collection of locally woven baskets on the shelf above the stove, and the needlepoint sampler over the sink that read BLESS THIS MESS.

"I didn't want the place to look sterile just because it's a government building," she said, clearing her throat.

He nodded. His glance swept over her with a look of appreciation tinged with puzzlement. She sensed that he was trying to piece together the information he'd gleaned from her kitchen and from her. She felt open to his inspection, far too open, and she turned back to the stove, away from his probing eyes. "You can wash up in the bathroom," she said.

When he returned, she was lighting two tapered candles on the table. "I keep them for power outages," she explained quickly, "but the power never goes out. I know candles don't spoil, but still . . ."

"No use taking a chance," Sean agreed readily, holding her chair out. He sat down across from Molly and raised his eyebrows when he saw the filled wineglasses.

Molly shrugged. "It was getting old sitting in the cupboard."

Sean's gaze fastened on her mouth as he raised his glass. "Then let's toast life's pleasures. They should be enjoyed before they grow too old — or before we do."

Molly's fingers tightened on the stem of her glass, but she raised it with a brief inclination of her head. "To life's pleasures," she murmured.

Candlelight and wine. She was beginning to wonder what strange impulse had prompted her to serve them up to Sean tonight. It must be her restless mood, the same feeling of wildness that had impelled her to wear the hoop earrings.

95

The meal was quiet, and Molly felt the room enveloping them in homey warmth. The oven clicked as it cooled, the candles sputtered, and Sean watched Molly over his wineglass.

"Why did you go into forestry?" he asked suddenly.

"I was one of those kids every parent dreads — a collector." She smiled at him. "I came home with leaves and insects and rocks and insisted on labeling each one and putting it on display in my bedroom. One day while my mother was dusting, she moved a shoebox and a toad jumped out at her. After that she refused to set foot in my room ever again." Sean laughed, and Molly found herself gazing at him hungrily. "Sue, on the other hand," she said, lowering her eyes to her plate, "owned the world's largest collection of Barbie dolls. Before he died my dad would take us to the woods to pick blackberries and she'd bring her dolls plus several changes of clothing for them and little combs for their hair." Molly watched the wine swirl in her glass as she slowly tilted it. "Sue's a terrific mom."

In the silence that followed, Sean said softly, "You and Steve didn't have any children."

Molly shook her head. "We were fighting

96

all the time. And I wanted my children to have a father. As it turned out, I made the right decision," she added.

Sean frowned down into his wineglass. "You must still think about having them." He shot her a measuring glance, and Molly shrugged. "You said I'd be good with a baby when I brought you Thoreau," he said quietly. "That's an observation generally made by someone who's thinking about babies herself."

"What a wonderful memory you have," she said dryly. "But what I said about wanting my children to have a father still stands. I won't build a home with a man who might not be there tomorrow." She met his gaze defiantly.

He set down his wineglass. "I know it's trite, but life offers no guarantees, Molly. People die every day from ordinary things like driving a car."

She didn't know if Sean was still talking about her marriage to Steve or about a possible relationship between the two of them, and she felt as if she were stranded on a mountaintop with a precipice on each side. On the one hand, she no longer felt capable of blocking Sean totally out of her life; on the other, she knew that if she let him in any further she'd be leaving herself wide open for pain and disappointment. Because a relationship with Sean Feyer would have to end someday.

"And some people live quiet lives," she said.

"Isn't that a quote from Thoreau?" he asked. "*Quiet lives of desperation.* I can't imagine you married to someone leading that kind of life, Molly."

"I can," she retorted, cutting the remainder of her meatloaf into tiny pieces to hide her agitation. For, in truth, she had been introduced to dozens of such men by her friends. She had even gone out with several of them. And she had found them all boring. What bothered her was the way Sean seemed to know that without being told. It made those imaginary precipices even more dangerous.

Sean didn't press his advantage. He turned back to a last spoonful of potatoes with a small lift of his shoulders that said it was really no concern of his, and Molly relaxed.

They finished the meal in silence, and she poured the remainder of the wine into their glasses before she started clearing the table. Sean carried his plate to the sink, and she saw him press a knuckle to his right eye as he turned back to the table.

"Is your eye hurting?" she asked hesitantly as she ran hot water into the sink to soak the meatloaf pan. Her eyes scanned his back anxiously.

He carried the rest of the dishes to the sink before replying. "I guess I'm a little tired," he finally admitted. "My vision's a bit more blurred than usual."

Molly idly swirled her hands in the water. She had imagined over and over what had happened the day Steve died. The road had been wet from a light rain. She had pictured a rainbow slick of oil on the blacktop. Steve had been going too fast as usual. And he hadn't been wearing a helmet. He'd taken a curve too fast, and the motorcycle had left the road. She blinked hard. She hadn't been there, but she could see it all as clearly as if she'd been right there on the cycle with him.

"Were you frightened when your plane crashed?" she asked suddenly, raising her eyes to his.

Carefully he set the plates on the counter next to the sink. She watched his eyes cloud and was reminded again of the smoke rolling through the verdant forest in the mountains. "There wasn't much time to be scared," Sean said, "but, yes, I suppose I was terrified. I really didn't have a chance to worry about it, though." He gave her a humorless smile, and his eyes swung to the window. Dusk had settled over the mountain, and he stared out into the darkness. "I was on an observation flight in an L-19. I was radioing the fire's progress to the fire boss on the ground when I spotted a tractor driver in trouble. He was trying to slash a fire wall, and it was obvious he'd become disoriented in the smoke. The tractor was moving almost in a circle, like a little yellow bug caught in a maze." Sean's eyes narrowed, and he was silent for a moment. "The fire had just exploded the tops of the pines ahead of the tractors, and the flames were curling back over it like some giant tidal wave ready to just crash down and devour that little tractor. I knew the guy was a goner unless I could get him reoriented. I radioed down and gave him directions to turn to a three o'clock position. He was new, and this was his first major fire. He was terrified too."

Molly's hands had stilled in the water and she couldn't take her eyes from Sean's face.

"The smoke rolled in over him, and I couldn't tell if he was following my directions or not. I banked the plane and flew down under the curl of fire. I'll never forget that." His voice was filled with awe. "It flashed through my head that I was flying

100

into Hades. My wingtips almost brushed the tops of the pines. I saw the tractor then. It was heading straight for the flames. I radioed again, and just when he got turned in the right direction I felt the plane start to vibrate from the turbulence . . ."

The silence stretched between them like a rope pulled taut. Molly couldn't move, couldn't tear her eyes away from Sean. His knuckles were powder white against the counter. "The tractor made it out all right," he said, a small smile touching the corners of his mouth, which were also pale with tension. "I don't really remember the crash. I just suddenly found that I was on the ground, dragging myself through the forest on my belly. My leg was broken, and I'd hit my head. I was lucky to come down beyond the fire line. Another plane radioed my position, and a ground crew picked me up an hour later."

Molly suddenly realized that she was shaking like a leaf. Unbidden tears pricked at the backs of her eyes. She pulled her hands from the water and dried them on a towel, her head lowered. She took a chocolate pie with whipped-cream topping from the refrigerator and set it on the counter. Her voice sounded unnaturally harsh when she spoke. "This needs to warm up a bit before we cut it. I just took it out of the freezer before I started dinner."

"Can I help?" Sean asked as she poured water into the coffeepot.

She shook her head. "No, everything's fine." But everything wasn't fine. Sean had breached the wall Molly had so carefully erected between them, and she was shaken. While he'd been telling her about his attempt to save the man on that yellow tractor, she had barely managed to stop herself from putting her arms around him. She was still aching from the desire to touch him, to ease some of his pain.

Abruptly she jerked the plastic bag of garbage from the can near the back door and twisted it closed with a plastic tie. "I'd better put this outside," she said, "before I forget. Gil always takes the trash for me. He'll be by in the morning." She couldn't seem to stop herself from babbling, as though she had just lived through his traumatic experience and her relief at being alive was overwhelming.

She hurried outside and plopped the bag into the metal trash can by the back door, then took a deep breath and closed her eyes. She heard the door open and close again, softly, and she stiffened when he stopped behind her.

"The stars are brilliant tonight," he murmured, and slowly Molly opened her eyes and looked up. They were indeed brilliant. "Look," he said, pointing over her shoulder at the southern sky. "There's the constellation Capricorn."

Molly followed his finger to the stars just above the horizon. "Think of the billions of people before us who saw that same constellation," she said. "They must have lived and loved and died beneath those very stars, one generation after another." Her voice was weary and tight.

Sean's hand dropped softly to her shoulder, his thumb caressing the nape of her neck. "It's a very faint constellation," he said quietly. "Look there to the left. That's where the German astronomer Johann Galle first observed Neptune in 1846. Neptune takes a hundred and sixty-five years to complete its trip around the sun, so it won't arrive back at the spot where it was first discovered until the year 2011."

"I never really think of the stars as moving," Molly said, a note of wonder creeping into her voice. A magical warmth was weaving its way through her veins as Sean traced a pattern on her neck, a pattern intricate as a map of the stars.

"The whole universe is in motion," Sean

said. "Revolving, spinning, changing. A long time from now the constellations we know today won't even be recognizable."

"It makes humanity seem pretty insignificant," Molly said, a deep sigh pressing against her heart.

"No," Sean said softly, and she could feel his warm breath on her neck. "We're very significant travelers on a planet moving through space. We're part of an immense cosmic voyage. Think how wonderful it is."

"You'd make a great celestial travel agent," she told him.

She sensed that he was smiling. The hand stroking her neck gently turned her around. Soft moonlight washed over his features, giving his flesh the look of marble statuary. If not for the glittering green eyes and enigmatic smile, Molly would have believed the night had turned him into a ghostly presence from the forest, but a presence invested with potent masculinity.

His voice was a caress in the dark. "The moon revolves around Earth, and Earth revolves around the sun. They're swirling through space locked in each other's gravitational pull, like an embrace." Sean gathered Molly to him very slowly, and her breath caught at the contact with his warm body. She felt like a planet being pulled into

Sean's orbit, a strong magnetism linking her irrevocably to him. His voice was a compelling whisper borne of the mystical depths of the forest that surrounded them. "Hear the music, Molly? It's the pines and the wind right here on our planet Earth, and it's just for us." His fingers on her spine made her ache for closer contact, and it was with difficulty that she kept from resting her head on his chest. He was so warm, so seductive, so inviting . . .

Hard reason had no place on a night like this, and all the negative voices inside her head were silenced by Sean's touch. It was as though a wave of mountain smoke had entered her soul, casting an enchanting spell. This was not a night for reality.

Humming softly, a love song, he guided her in a slow dance under the moon and the stars — and Molly yielded to the magic. The pine needles were their dance floor, the stars their crystal chandelier, and the whispering pines their orchestra. They danced under the canopy of trees, in and out of shadows. Sean's fingers played lightly over her back and down her hips, and she molded her body to his, matching his sinuous dance movements with breathless precision. Her hips brushed against his, their thighs pressed together, and Molly twined her arms around Sean's neck, pressing one palm against the coarse hair at the nape of his neck. His green eyes glittered like the pines as moonlight flashed across them. Somewhere a lone whippoorwill warbled desolately, and Molly's heartbeat pounded inside her veins . . . She couldn't remember when they had stopped dancing, but now they stood under the bough of a pine tree, the moon cupping their faces like a celestial hand. Molly swallowed convulsively as she stared into Sean's face. A low drone in the sky insinuated itself into the night, and slowly Molly tore her eyes away from him and looked up. Over the pinnacles of the mountains came a small plane, its red and green lights winking ceremoniously. The image crossed Molly's consciousness like an omen, a hawk flying across the moon. It forced her to remember why she couldn't let Sean touch her like this, why she couldn't let herself feel this way in his arms.

Abruptly she shivered.

"You're cold?" he asked at once.

She nodded, staring down at the shadows on the ground. "I'd better go in. I don't know how all those stars keep from freezing to death," she added, trying for levity.

She must have succeeded in striking the right chord because Sean smiled and put his arm around her shoulders as he guided her back to the house. He glanced up at the disappearing plane, and she felt his arm tighten.

"I love flying at night," he said softly. "I see a lone pinpoint of light there on the ground in the darkness, and I know there's a house below me, and someone is waiting for someone else to come home. Or the family is together inside. It makes me feel good."

She smiled tightly. Nothing about planes made her feel good, not where Sean was concerned.

The plane had cast a pall on her mood, but she didn't have much time to think about it, because the moment she entered the kitchen she saw Thoreau staring up at her from the counter. He was hunched over the chocolate cream pie, which was now an unrecognizable blob. The foil pie plate was balanced precariously at the edge of the counter, and Thoreau was thoroughly covered with whipped cream. It dripped from his whiskers. It dripped from his little black nose. And it dripped from his paws.

"Thoreau!" Molly wailed, running toward him. With the instinct of a child caught with his hand in the cookie jar, the raccoon turned and scurried to the end of the counter, skittering on his cream-coated paws and sliding full tilt into the electric coffee-maker. The jolt was enough to jar the remains of the pie, and as Thoreau clambered down from the counter via the towel rack, the pie plate flipped onto the floor, splattering whipped cream and chocolate filling across the tile like so many dollops of thick paint.

Molly turned plaintive eyes on Sean. But as he stared back, clearly startled by the whole scene, a slow smile began to spread across Molly's face. An answering quirk turned up the corners of Sean's mouth, and Molly felt the first bubbling of helpless laughter deep in her throat. Sean's chuckle joined hers, and a moment later they dissolved in full-fledged hilarity. They leaned against the counter on their elbows, holding their heads in their hands, laughing till they cried. "I've never seen such a mess," Molly howled in a gale of giggles.

"He's a master of destruction," Sean agreed, wiping a tear from his cheek. His smile was crooked, and the green eyes watching her had turned dusky.

Molly's laughter died away, and her heart raced faster as she stared back at him. The moonlight-etched shadows on his face had given way here in the kitchen to warm planes and hollows burnished by the dim overhead light. Her skin still glowed with the remembered feel of his body against hers. She dropped her eyes to the filthy floor and cleared her throat. "I guess I'd better clean this up." She tore off some paper towels and knelt to mop up their intended dessert. Sean squatted down opposite her and pushed some of the filling back into the pie pan, then carried it to the trash bag and dumped it in. By the time he sank down opposite her again she had almost completed the job and was going over the floor with a clean paper towel. "It's a shame, really," she said, not looking at him. "As store-bought frozen pies go, this one looked pretty good."

"It loses something on the floor," Sean agreed, but Molly could tell he didn't give a darn for the pie or the floor. She flushed when she looked up and found herself staring directly into the handsome face less than a foot from her own.

A tightness was growing inside her, a spring wound too far. She pressed her fist to the base of her throat to ease the coil of tension there, and swiftly Sean reached for her hand, pulling it to his mouth to brush it with his lips. The paper towels fell from her other hand and lay forgotten on the floor. Sean drew her to him, between his knees, and he stroked her hair back from her face. He touched her forehead with his lips, and she closed her eyes dreamily. Her hands sought and clutched the soft fabric of his shirt, palms unfolding to press the hardness of his chest.

He breathed warmly into her ear, and his tongue traced the whorls there. Molly's breath hissed inward through her teeth. As his mouth trailed downward, tasting the slender column of her neck, his hands lifted her sweater from her stomach and his thumbs made lazy circles just below her ribs. He leaned his head back to look at her, and through pleasure-glazed eyes Molly stared back, registering the fiercely possessive expression on his face. Through a gathering haze of torpid sensuality, she touched her hand to his face and hungrily stroked the hard line of his jaw, her thumb sliding to his lower lip. His lips parted and he nibbled on her thumb, his whispered words drumming against her skin. "Molly," he whispered, kissing her palm. "Beautiful Molly."

She slid her hand into his shirt, reveling in the touch of the springy hair on his chest. She could feel the heavy thudding of his heart. With languid slowness he shifted up her sweater to reveal her breasts, china white and smooth in the slightly bluish kitchen light. His thumbs strummed pink nipples to hard awareness before his mouth slipped down to take possession.

Desire had been a cold river inside her until now, sluggish and unnoticed. But it blazed into life at his intimate kiss, the river becoming a molten flow, thick and sweet, making her limbs heavy with longing. Dear Lord. She had never even guessed herself capable of this intense need for one particular man. It was completely alien to her nature. It was unexplainable by all the mathematical facts and probabilities she knew. It was like stepping deeper into the forest and suddenly stumbling upon a hot, jungle paradise. But this paradise was in her soul, and it was Sean who'd led her to it.

But paradise was a state of mind totally alien to Molly, and she was reluctant to accept it now. It occurred to her that she was becoming involved with Sean through no conscious effort on her part. It was as though some indefinable part of herself was reaching out to him. He had come to her unbidden, and now so did this desire flaring inside her. She didn't know how to deal with it.

Her hands withdrew from his shirt and he looked up at her, startled by the sudden withdrawal. She stared back expressionlessly. It was too much too soon. She wasn't ready.

She saw the glitter in his eyes harden. Don't say anything about Steve or I'll start crying, she warned him silently. Not from grief, she thought, but from confusion.

Gently he pulled her sweater back in place, his eyes still on her face, and Molly wanted to explain, but she couldn't find the words.

"I want you, Molly," he whispered. "Not just like this, the heat of the moment in your kitchen. I want you in my bed and in my life."

It wasn't what she'd expected to hear. "Sean, I need some time," she said slowly. "I'm not ready for everything this fast."

"And you're not ready for someone who earns his living the way I do," he added softly.

She shook her head to clear it. In so many ways he reminded her of Steve. Reminded her, yet didn't. What he'd said earlier was true: One hour alone with him and she'd never again confuse him with her dead husband. She flushed at the memory and gave up a small smile.

"You're as tough to root out of one's life as a wild rose bush," she grudgingly complained. "And twice as thorny."

"Do you want me out of your life?" he asked, his eyes probing her face, and no doubt reading all the uncertainty and loneliness she was too weary to hide.

"Unfair question," she said quickly, pushing herself onto her heels and standing up. She turned her back on him and brushed off her slacks.

Sean's hand on Molly's shoulder was insistent as he turned her around to face him, and she felt herself shiver at the determination she read in his face. His cheekbones were hard silvery ridges in the dim light, his eyes green stars. "This is your chance, Molly," he said quietly. "I may not give you another one. Tell me now if you don't want me in your life."

"You're being unfair, Sean," she protested, but he was unwavering. And he was right. This was the time to stop what was happening between them before their involvement deepened. This was the time when it wouldn't hurt . . . at least not too much. She stared at him and slowly expelled her breath. "No," she said softly. "I don't want you out of my life."

She saw the tension leave his face and body then, and a crooked smile lifted one edge of his mouth. "Good night, gorgeous," he said teasingly, his finger tracing a line down her nose. He planted a gentle kiss on her forehead. "Don't go dancing out in the moonlight without me."

She watched from the kitchen doorway as he left. He paused a moment by the end table in the living room to examine the chunk of pyrite. He hefted it once, put it back, and with a backward glance over his shoulder, he gave her a smile and walked out the door.

Chapter 5

Molly took a bite of her tuna-salad sandwich and leaned back against the rhododendron trunk. Autumn had painted the mountains with the vivid palette of a Van Gogh. In the valleys below, an orange splash of pumpkins showed against the pale dried brown of cornstalks. She loved this time of year.

The sounds were unique to the season: dried leaves skittering along the ground, squirrels chattering as they stored nuts for winter, the whistling of . . . Whistling? She sat up straighter and stared hard at the thick stand of pines from which the sound was coming. A second later the underbrush crackled and parted and Sean strode out into the clearing to face Molly. He was Henry David Thoreau in the flesh as he stopped and grinned at her. Dried twigs and leaves clung to his tight blue jeans, and his sweatshirt sported a tear at the shoulder. He'd clearly taken the scenic route in. He swung his pack off his shoulder, set down a guitar — a guitar?! — and came toward her with his walking stick in hand.

"Good afternoon," he called cheerily, throwing the pack down beside her, sinking to the ground, and leaning back against the tree.

"Just happened to be in the neighborhood?" Molly asked casually.

"Silly one. I live in the forest. Didn't you know that?" He was unpacking his knapsack, pulling out cheese and fruit and French bread while Molly stared.

"I can just picture you nestled in the top of a pine," Molly said. "You and the squirrels."

Sean grinned and dropped a paper plate in her lap, which he proceeded to load with delicacies from his pack. "Actually, I think you'd like my house," he said. "The welcome mat's out anytime you want to visit."

"What's it like?" she asked, pretending to study the cheese on her plate.

"Like a lovely chalet overlooking a small lake," he said at once, spreading hot mustard on the bread and topping it with a thick slice of cheese. "It's nestled against the side of a mountain. I've got a little trout stream and rumors of black bear on the property." He took a bite of the bread and then continued. "Take the old highway toward Asheville and turn to the north when you see a big waterfall and a small power plant. My place is about a half-mile up that road."

He crunched a big bite from an apple and set the fruit on his plate. Picking up his guitar, he began to strum softly. Molly felt an odd heat suffuse her body as she remembered the way those fingers had strummed her bare flesh. He hummed along as he played, throwing her an occasional smile, and Molly gave in to the enchanted mood he was creating. If she had dreamed up the perfect fall afternoon, she couldn't have done any better than this reality. She studied Sean covertly as she picked at the rest of her cheese and fruit. Just when she thought she had him pegged, he went and did something like this and she had to totally rearrange her notions about him.

When he'd finished the song, she applauded softly and said, "Very nice. I had no idea you were a musician."

"A barely passable one," he said. "But I couldn't think of any way to import a full string section up here for lunch."

"You do have a way of creating ambience," she admitted, indicating the plate of food and his guitar with a wave of her hand.

"I have to," he said. "You're a difficult

lady to court. I can't just whisk you out of the forest and into a swanky French restaurant for chateaubriand and champagne." He gestured at the forest and said, "You have your arboreal duties to perform."

Molly glanced at her watch. "Speaking of which . . ."

Sean sighed and stood up. "Walk me to the trail." Without waiting for her answer, he gathered up his gear and clasped her hand in his, tugging her along with him. "There might be monsters lurking in the woods," he said with mock terror. "Best not to travel alone."

"We all have our demons," Molly interspersed, only half joking.

"Don't we though . . ." Sean's smile as he turned to face her was intimate and enigmatic. He pulled her into his arms, wrapping them around her for warmth, and rested his chin on her head. "Let me slay your demons for you, Molly," he whispered, planting a soft kiss on her hair. Before she could answer, he lifted his head, tilted her chin up, and brought his lips down on hers. She found herself melting against him before she even knew what she was doing. But it was Sean who pulled away first, only his crooked smile and rapid breathing betraying his emotions. "Look," he said, pointing to a twig on a nearby bush. Molly turned her head in the arc of his arm, still leaning against his chest, and saw a dried, dark brown curl that looked like a dead leaf. "A swallowtail pupa," Molly said, smiling. "Wouldn't that be lovely, to curl up and sleep like that for winter, then turn into a butterfly the next spring?"

Sean was watching her expression with an indefinable light in his eyes, and Molly fell silent. "It would indeed," he agreed softly with that curious half-smile. "But I think we all undergo similar changes all the time — at least on the inside." He touched her chin with his finger and adjusted the pack on his back. When he looked at her again, there was laughter in his eyes. "I'll see you to-night."

She watched him walk down the trail, forcing herself not to ask what he had planned for tonight. Sean Feyer was full of surprises. She turned back to the bush as he disappeared from sight and stared at the swallowtail pupa. For some reason it made her think of the trench where Sean had held her while fire raged overhead. Some kind of metamorphosis she didn't fully compre-hend had begun in that trench, and it was still going on. She lifted her arms and whim-sically inspected them. No wings yet.

★ ★ ★

An olive-drab truck with the Forest Service insignia on the door was parked in front of the station when Molly got back, and she sat in the jeep a minute after turning off the ignition. Then she went to greet her visitor.

Mart Connelson was a middle-aged man with a long face that made it look as though his chin weighed five pounds and had stretched his head with its weight. Bushy white hair matched bushy white eyebrows, and as Molly approached the porch she saw that the clear blue eyes held an almost birdlike excitement today. Mart stood up from the chair and extended his hand. "Congratulations, Molly, I heard you handled that fire real well."

"Thank you, Mr. Connelson." She shook his hand and gestured toward the door. "Would you like some coffee?"

She held her breath as he followed her inside. He paused to examine Thoreau's hollow log, and Molly explained about the raccoon and added that he was locked in an animal cage when she was gone. Mr. Connelson nodded, and Molly went on to the kitchen. What did the district supervisor want here? Had something gone wrong with the timber contract?

They talked of trees and fires while she

made the coffee, and Molly grew more restive. By the time she finally set the mugs on the table and took the seat opposite him she had imagined all kinds of disasters.

Connelson sat back with his coffee and smiled at her over the steam. "I've been getting some very good feedback from the public relations work you've done lately, Molly. Several people sent us complimentary notes about your talk at the businesswomen's club."

"Thank you." This didn't sound like it was leading up to a disaster, but she still had an uneasy feeling . . .

Connelson had evidently savored the suspense long enough. He rocked forward to the table and set down his coffee. "We're very pleased with your work. Your talents and experience make you a real asset to the Forest Service, Molly." He smiled at her and laced his hands over the coffee cup. "We're moving you up, Molly. A staff position in Asheville will be opening up soon, and we're assigning you there."

"A staff position?" she repeated thickly, not yet fully comprehending his words. "You mean I won't be working here anymore?" Her mind kicked into gear and began racing with the implications of this new "promotion."

"That's right. We feel you've had enough field work. You're well trained, and you've shown tremendous leadership ability. You'll be supervising a staff of five in Asheville. The job opens up in just two months." His brows suddenly knitted together, and the blue eyes regarded her in puzzlement. "Is something wrong, Molly? Is there a problem here?"

She sighed and stood up, running a hand through her hair. "It's not that I don't appreciate the opportunity and your confidence in me," she said, picking her words carefully. She leaned her hands on the back of her chair and faced him directly. "I'm very happy here, Mr. Connelson. I've found that I love the field work."

Connelson slowly rubbed his hands together over the coffee, then frowned and took a thoughtful sip. "Molly," he said, a note of sympathy in his voice, "the staff position is a substantial promotion. Do you realize how important it could be to your career?"

Her fingers tightened on the chair and then she pushed herself away and paced the kitchen in agitation. "A staff position means a desk and a lot of papers and an apartment in the city. The closest I'll get to a forest is the stack of papers that used to be a tree before it was cut for pulp. I'm not suited to that kind of life, Mr. Connelson." She shook her head vehemently and stopped pacing to face him, her arms crossed over her chest.

Connelson slowly shook his head and ran a hand over his eyes. "I'm sorry, Molly. But we can't leave you here indefinitely. It's not fair to the young foresters who want a chance to learn in the field. They need to take over for you here. But most of all, it's not fair to you. You deserve to move up in the organization. Come on." He gave her a hopeful smile. "I'm sure you'll like it once you get settled in at Asheville."

He stood up, and she realized he was dismissing her objections. She moved toward the table and tried one more time. "I love working in the forest, Mr. Connelson." When she recognized the resolution in his eyes, she brought her hand down on the table, hard, stinging her palm. "You can't take away this life I've learned to love!"

"I'm sorry, Molly," he said quietly, walking toward the door. "We have to follow procedures for advancement. If you're dead set on remaining in the field, the only thing I can suggest is a commercial timber grower." She had trailed after him helplessly, and he stopped at the front door. "Think it over

123

carefully," he said, giving her an encouraging smile, "and let me know what you decide. We want to keep you in the Forest Service, Molly."

Molly nodded shortly. "I'll let you know. Thank you for stopping by." She watched as he got in his truck and pulled away. What a bittersweet day this has been, she thought.

Molly was still standing on the porch staring out at the trees when Gil pulled up in his jeep. "You okay?" he asked, hopping out.

"Hmm?" She looked at him, still frowning, and realized she hadn't heard what he said. "Mart Connelson was just here."

"Yeah, I passed his truck on the road. What's up?"

"He's giving me a staff job in Asheville." She turned and started back inside the station.

"Hey, that's great!" Gil said, following her. "What's the problem?"

Molly threw her hands in the air and sank down at the kitchen table. "Paperwork, a stuffy office, the city — that's the problem."

"Hell, Molly, that's what it's all about. Working your way up. We all know that. Field work is just training."

Molly shook her head in exasperation. "But, dammit, I like working in the forest."

Gil ran his hand through hair the color of

red maple leaves. Slowly he sat down at the kitchen table opposite her. "I don't know, Molly. It never occurred to me that you'd object to being promoted. I guess there's not much you can do about it, though. Why don't you just try the job and see how things go? You'll probably adjust just fine and fit right in."

Gil's tone was as sympathetic as Mart Connelson's had been — and as puzzled. She knew that neither man was capable of understanding her deep-rooted affinity for the forest. Abruptly she pushed herself away from the table and snatched up her running shoes from the counter by the door. "Those notes you wanted on the beetle problem are on my desk," she said as she leaned against the counter to tie the shoes. "I need to get out and run a little."

"Okay," Gil said. "I'll take them with me to study. Have a good run."

"Thanks, Gil." Molly was already halfway out the door. She started to jog even before she reached the dirt road, making her feet pound out a steady, hard rhythm, keeping time with the words pounding in her head: *paperwork . . . desk job . . . bureaucracy.*

She followed the old logging road leading deeper into the forest, running flat out now. It was ironic how things worked. Gil, a for-

125

estry aide, was training in the forest, and he could hardly wait to get a laboratory job where he could sit inside and research tree diseases. Molly, on the other hand, had been doing exactly what she loved, caring for every aspect of the living forest. And now, as her reward for a job well done, she would be relegated to a desk. She'd known how the system worked when she entered forestry school, but she hadn't realized how deeply she'd come to love the trees themselves, all grace and permanence and beauty. Lord knows, there had been precious little permanence in her childhood or her marriage. These trees had come to represent something she'd never gotten from her family, a real sense of stability.

Here in the forest Molly came closest to experiencing a feeling of completeness, a sense of life as a continuing spectrum. Here in the forest that lonely corner of her heart found something that was lacking in the rest of her life. And yet the void never totally disappeared. It just didn't hurt as much when the pines were whispering overhead and the sun was warming her face.

Life marched on in the forest, against all odds, and Molly drew on that indomitable spirit. When she ran like this the painful isolation dropped away like so many pieces of extraneous clothing left strewn on the path behind her. In its place tonight there was just cold anger at the threatened loss of her life's wellspring, the forest.

Molly reached the mile-and-a-half point on the road and stopped to take deep, gulping breaths while she braced herself against an old tulip tree, her fingers curling over the thick, ridged bark. She stared upward at the straight trunk, then pushed off forcefully and began jogging back. Most of her anger had abated, but the sense of frustration was still there.

Her pace was slower, her breathing less ragged, but her eyes remained hard. The evening air was humid, and the smoke drifting lazily just above her head failed to enchant her tonight.

He came out of the smoke ahead, the way he always seemed to, his face creasing into a grin when he saw her. He had on his usual jeans with a light blue sweat shirt, and he was jogging toward her. She felt suddenly resentful of his presence here on her mountain, in her forest. Her moodiness deepened.

Sean slowed and turned, falling into step with her as she drew alongside him. "I figured you were jogging when I stopped by the station and you were gone." He cast her a sideways glance when she didn't answer. Molly tightened her mouth, breathing sharply through her nose. They ran silently the rest of the way back, dusk chasing them with its gray veil. The smoke was still rolling in when they reached the ranger station, and dew hung heavily on the grass and trees. Sean had stopped by his truck, but Molly ran all the way up the station steps, shoving the door open and letting it slam behind her.

She kicked off her damp shoes and went to the back room to let Thoreau out of his cage. He headed straight for his hollow log in the living room while Molly went to the kitchen. She had it in mind to fix herself a salad, but instead she found herself banging cupboard doors in futile activity.

She steeled herself when she heard the front door open and close again, and she sensed Sean standing in the kitchen doorway. "It's been a rotten day," she muttered before he could speak, without turning to look at him. "And to top it off I can't find the damn lettuce." She balled her fists on the counter, staring morosely at her reflection in the toaster.

"Did you by any chance have it out on the counter this morning?" he asked quietly.

She nodded. "I thought I put it back, right

128

after I locked Thoreau in his cage . . ." Her voice trailed off, and she turned to Sean to find him nodding.

"I saw half a head of lettuce strewn around his log," he confirmed. "Shall I beat him or would you like to do it?"

The utter seriousness of his tone coupled with the sympathy in his eyes undid her. She began to smile. "I'm sorry. It really has been a rotten day."

"Want to talk about it?"

She shook her head, but gave him a grateful smile. "Not right now."

"Okay." He put his hands on his hips and surveyed the kitchen. Then he went to Molly and, guiding her by the shoulders, sat her down in a chair. "Any more wine?" he asked hopefully. When she shook her head, he bit his lower lip and thought for a moment. "Well, I'll have to make do," he said finally, striding toward the refrigerator.

Sean's "making do" involved the conjuring up of a wonderful drink made with apple juice, pineapple juice, a fresh-squeezed orange, and a dash of grenadine syrup he found. He also managed to put together a pretty terrific omelet with cheddar cheese, grated potato, and onion. "This is gourmet fare," she teased him. "I bet your Ivy League education included a cooking course or two along the way."

"I picked up a lot of things along the way," he said, "but gourmet cooking wasn't included. Personally, I think you're so hungry right now that a cardboard box would taste good."

She settled back with a smile, digging into her omelet and stealing a glance across the table at Sean's leonine features. She was rapidly falling back under his spell.

They sat in the living room after dinner, and Sean brought out the stack of books he'd carried in for her, all science fiction. He coaxed a fire out of the old logs she hadn't touched in a year, and they settled back on the couch, at opposite ends. Sean strummed his guitar and hummed and Molly found herself propping her stockinged feet up on the couch, nearly toe-to-toe with his. Thoreau insisted on playing the hyperactive child in this tableau of domesticity, barreling up the couch to inspect their feet and hurtling himself off when Sean tickled his belly with a toe.

Molly felt surprisingly warm and relaxed. Sean had effectively taken her mind off the staff position in Asheville. She thought of mentioning it to him now that she felt calmer, but rejected the idea. It was her problem, after all, and no concern of his.

"I almost forgot," Sean suddenly said, laying his guitar on the floor. "Look what I found today." She sat up and hugged her knees to her chest, watching as he fished through his pockets, a look of boyish enthusiasm on his face. He pulled out a rock and displayed it proudly on the flat of his hand. Molly gasped when it caught the light. It was bright green, a crystal of some kind, almost three inches long. It looked like a magical miniature obelisk.

"It's beautiful," she said, taking the rock from him and turning it over carefully.

"It's olivine," Sean said, "also called chrysolite or peridot. I have a couple of samples at home, but nothing like this. The crystals are rare, and to find one this large is extraordinary."

Molly was warmed by the pride in his voice. She found it difficult to tear her gaze from the olivine, which was the exact shade of Sean's eyes. "Where did you find it?" she asked.

"That same spot near the waterfall where I found the pyrite," he said. "I used the pick on some metamorphosed dolomite. When I cracked it apart, there was the crystal — as if it were just waiting to be discovered."

Molly listened with a quiet smile while Sean rambled on about various rock formations and what was likely to be found in them. Her mind was on the waterfall, and she stared down at the crystal in her hand as if she could actually see the forest reflected in its rich green light. "Basalt . . . igneous rocks high in magnesium . . . gabbro . . ." Snatches of Sean's lecture penetrated her brain, but most of her attention was focused on the faceted green rock that was bewitching her the way Sean's eyes did.

She looked up guiltily when she realized he had fallen silent. Her hand was absently caressing the olivine and she glanced at it wryly. "It really is beautiful," she said, handing it back to him.

"You know, green is your color," he said, looking at the rock and then at her. "It accents those blue eyes of yours and that lovely black hair . . ." His voice trailed off, and she stared back at him, feeling her heart pounding in increased agitation. It briefly flashed through Molly's mind that she wanted Sean to spend the night. It was cold outside and a little lonely, and he made her forget about everything but the warmth of his touch and what that did to her pulse. She met his eyes fiercely, inviting him, asking and wanting him. He leaned toward her, his mouth grown serious, lashes veiling his gaze. Molly caught her breath.

They both jumped when they heard the crash in the bedroom. Sean leaped up first, and Molly followed close on his heels. She nearly plowed into his back when he halted just inside her bedroom door. Molly peered around him and muttered, "Thoreau. I might have known."

Sean shot her a rueful glance over his shoulder and bent to pick up the raccoon, who was trying to paw his way out of an enormous pile of sweaters and odds and ends that he'd apparently knocked off the top shelf of Molly's closet. Molly quickly knelt and began refolding the items of clothing. As she picked up one sweater, something fell to the floor with a heavy *clunk*. Molly looked down and saw a large piece of dull brass-colored metal.

Hurriedly she picked it up, feeling her stomach lurch. She started to wrap it in the sweater, and it clanked as it hit another piece of metal.

"What's that?" Sean asked, reaching to take the sweater from her. "Do you hide your valuable heirlooms in your sweaters?" One glance at her face, and his smile faded.

He set Thoreau on the floor and knelt beside her, thigh to thigh. Carefully he unwrapped the sweater. Molly's heart felt as cold and hard as the metal in his hands.

"It was one of Steve's trophies for motor-cycle racing," she said.

"Well, it used to be," Sean said, turning the pieces over. The base had tarnished and chipped, and the green felt on the bottom was half peeled away. The top part, with the motorcycle, was in even worse shape. A large chunk was missing from the bike, and the remainder was black and green with corrosion. "This could be fixed," he said softly. When he looked at her face, he frowned. "Molly, what's wrong?"

"I don't want it fixed," she said roughly. She jerked the broken trophy and sweater away from him, and something else dropped to the floor. Sean picked it up and held it to the light. His eyes were glittering with confusion when they swung to her. "Molly?"

She looked unwillingly at the wedding ring in his hand and felt her heart constrict painfully. The ring was almost as badly damaged as the trophy, its shape no longer perfectly symmetrical, its gold color dull and lifeless. "Let me have it back," she said, reaching for the ring.

Sean handed it to her, but his fingers closed over her hand when she had the ring on her palm. "Talk to me, Molly," he said almost fiercely. "What happened to these things?"

Molly pulled her hand out of Sean's grip and balled her fists around the ring and the sweater with the trophy pieces. "I came home after Steve's funeral and packed up all of his things," she said in a tight voice, staring down at the sweater. "I stuck everything in boxes and set them outside. Then I called the junk man." She dared a glance at Sean and saw his eyes searching her face. "It rained the night before he came," she said. "Some of the boxes fell apart and the contents spilled onto the driveway. When the man came he loaded up most of it, but after he'd gone I found the trophy and the ring on the ground. They were all dented. I started to throw them in the wastebasket, but then I decided to keep them."

"It's all right, honey," he said in a low voice, cupping her chin and turning her to face him. "It must have hurt to throw those things away. I'm just sorry they were smashed like this."

Molly shook her head. "You don't understand, Sean. These don't have any sentimental value to me." She dropped the things on the floor. She squared her shoulders and stood up, crossing her arms. "I keep the ring and trophy as reminders of a bad mistake I don't intend to repeat. I won't get involved with another man like Steve."

135

She could see him in the mirror on her dresser as he stood up with the sweater in his hands. "That's crazy, Molly," he said softly.

It crossed her mind that one move and Sean would take her in his arms and hold her. And she would willingly walk into the same trap she'd fallen into once before.

"It's crazy," she said with quiet finality. "I'm human, Sean. Sometimes I forget what it was like. But when I look at that ring or that trophy, I remember. I can't recall Steve as clearly now, but I can still remember exactly how that marriage felt."

"Even memory gets distorted." His voice was sharp, and Molly smiled without humor.

"I don't know. Maybe it does. It doesn't really matter now."

She tensed when she saw him take a step toward her and then stop. "You're forgetting something very important," he said softly. "I'm not Steve."

"You take the same risks he did," she said, and spun around to face him. "Look at this trophy, Sean. You should have seen what Steve's motorcycle looked like after the accident." Her voice was breaking. "And Lord knows what he looked like. I can't deal with all of that again. I know what it means to be involved with a man like you, how it ends."

He reached out and touched her shoulder, his jaw tightening at the look of pain that flickered across her face despite her best efforts to contain her feelings.

From the corner of her eye she could see them in the mirror, facing each other like two strong trees, not quite touching and unable to move.

"You reached out the other night when you said you still wanted to see me," he said in a hard voice. "And now you're pulling back inside your wall again, Molly, shoring up your defenses and fending off the world. You were never meant to shut yourself off like that. You're a vital woman. You're alive, Molly. Only you won't allow yourself even that." His hand moved slowly to her neck and stroked the throbbing pulse there. Gently he shook his head. "Maybe I should have left the other night, when I still had the chance. Then we wouldn't both be caught here now, with this wall you've put between us." His hand moved up over her chin and traced the outline of her lips, and her breathing became labored. With his eyes still fastened on hers, he rolled the sweater into a ball around the trophy and ring and tossed it onto her bed. "Good night, Molly."

He was gone before she could make her wooden legs move or her misty eyes focus.

When she looked around the room, she really saw it for the first time. The thick rug and comforter were stark white. Her dresser was topped only by her cosmetics tray and the small shelf that held her meager rock collection. There were no flowers in this room, no pictures, no adornments. The table beside her bed held nothing but a small lamp, not even a pretty lamp she realized, and a plain wind-up alarm clock. She hugged her arms to herself and blinked hard. It was, she knew now, a sterile room; and its overpowering message was *Do Not Disturb*.

In one swift movement she crossed to the bed and swept the sweater and its contents onto the floor. The clatter sent Thoreau scurrying from the room.

Chapter 6

For three days she told herself she didn't miss Sean. For three days she expected to see him come walking out of the smoke on the mountains. She strained her ears for his whistle each day at lunch, and when it didn't come she lost her appetite and put her sandwich back in her pack. She kept glancing over her shoulder while jogging until she nearly ran head-on into a formidably large pine. She leaped up from the couch in the evening when she thought she heard the crunch of tires on gravel. But it was only the wind. Or the rain. Or a pine cone dropping in the forest.

Like hell she didn't miss him.

The third night she did hear a car outside, but when she opened the door, fighting to tame a too-ready smile, she saw it was her sister, Sue. "Oh, it's you."

"Thanks a lot. I can see you're thrilled by my visit."

"Sorry. Come on in." Molly stood aside,

taking one last hopeful look out the door before she closed it.

"Something's bothering you," Sue observed, tossing her purse in the general direction of the couch. The purse hit the floor, but Sue sank down on the couch, stretching her legs out straight and leaning her head back.

"What makes you say that?" Molly asked with a weak smile. "Want some tea?"

"Mmm, sounds good." Sue pushed herself off the couch and followed Molly to the kitchen. "Have you forgotten, darling?" she demanded, dropping wearily onto a kitchen chair. "I have two children, and they both possess *the family trait.*"

"That sounds ominous," Molly said, laughing. "Now what is this family curse?"

"No, no. Not a curse. A trait. The Carter family pout."

"This sounds like a dandy," Molly said, leaning back against the counter while she waited for the water to boil.

"It's true," Sue protested. "Honest. Your lower lip sticks out just like Trev's does when something goes wrong." She cast a critical eye on Molly. "And I'd say that whatever's happened is pretty serious. Does it have anything to do with Sean?"

Molly took a deep breath and sat down

140

with two cups of tea. "Sean found my wedding ring and an old trophy of Steve's."

Sue sighed. "And he thinks you're hung up on the past."

"In a way." Molly shrugged. "I told him I kept the stuff as a reminder not to get involved with anyone like Steve again."

"Apparently that didn't sit well."

Molly shook her head ruefully. "I know how different Sean is from Steve." She stopped and frowned. "And yet there are some things that are the same. I can't even deal with the thought of losing someone again, not after Dad and then Steve. Do you think I'm being too defensive?"

Sue shrugged. "I don't really know. But I always got the feeling there was something unresolved with you after Steve died."

Molly stared off into space, her eyes fixed on the pot rack on the wall but not seeing it.

"Like when Dad died," Sue ventured softly. Molly swung her eyes to her sister, a troubled look on her face. "I can remember the two of us lying in bed one night at Gram's," Sue said. "Before we got split up and sent to different houses. You pulled the covers up real tight to your chin and you said you were never going to get married and have a family because someone would die and it would hurt too much. You had that same expression on your face at Steve's funeral."

"I don't remember that night at Gram's," Molly said, staring down at the table.

"Honey, we don't remember a lot of things that aren't very pleasant. I was lucky. Aunt Sophie took me in. But you got booted from one house to another. It's no wonder you grew up so independent."

Molly absently swirled the spoon in her tea. "Maybe I should go see him," she murmured, half to herself. When she glanced up, Sue was smiling at her.

"First sensible thing you've said today," Sue declared. "Now drag out some cookies and I'll bore you with cute stories about the kids."

When Friday night came, Molly decided the time was ripe. She would make the first move.

She drove her own car, an ancient relic that wheezed but managed to hold paint job and soul together most of the time. She drove toward Asheville and found the waterfall and power plant Sean had told her about. She slowed the car at the turn and admired the view of rushing water visible through a curtain of dense blackberry bushes. She took the old road on up the mountain as it snaked past the power plant and wound its way beneath a thick arch of rhododendron.

She turned a corner and caught her breath as she saw his house. It was a red-wood A-frame, its solid glass front mir-roring the last golden rays of the sun, which were reflected on the large lake spread out below it. A stillness had settled over the mountain and over the tall pines clustered behind the house.

There were three other cars in the drive-way behind Sean's truck, and she hesitantly smoothed her pink silk blouse and red wool skirt as she got out of the car.

She watched Sean's face change as he opened the door, felt her throat relax when his eyes turned from emerald ice to warm sea green and a spontaneous grin warmed his features.

"Hi," Molly said awkwardly.

"I'm so glad you came," he murmured as he enveloped her in his arms.

Molly rested her head against his chest, and everything suddenly felt right. She looked up when he turned her around, feeling self-conscious in his protective em-brace when she saw the three men seated around a card table. Her eyes scanned the room quickly, taking in the large, open-beamed living room with modular couch and glass coffee tables on a thick brown carpet. The air was rank with cigar smoke and the smell of flat beer. The empty cans lay like toppled soldiers on the floor, a few wayward potato chips scattered among them.

Sean tugged her toward the table, calling out, "Fellows, I want you to meet Molly. She's a very special lady, so be nice to her." The boisterous laughter at the table quieted as three pairs of eyes swung in her direction.

Murmured assent went around the table. "You've been hiding this one away from us," one of the fellows accused Sean. "And no wonder. She's a real prize."

"By the way," a black-haired man in a flight jacket interjected, "do you always carry her under your arm like that? Or did you manage to glue yourself to her?"

Molly felt Sean's smile against her cheek as his lips grazed her there, and his hold relaxed slightly. "Glue. Now there's an idea." His fingers at her waist were spreading fire through her blood. "The loudmouth there is Rod," Sean announced, indicating the man in the flight jacket, and Rod gave her a nod and a fleeting smile. The other two were Breck and Dave. And, Sean said, all three were fire pilots.

Sean ushered Molly to the table, pulling

up an extra chair for her, and she sat down in a daze. Dave was shuffling the cards, and he insisted on dealing Molly in on the next hand. She stared sightlessly at her cards as Dave explained the rules of poker, specifically five-card draw. Rod opened a beer and pushed it over to her. Molly recoiled slightly from the plate of lunchmeat, cheese, and bread that was being passed around along with a plate of dill pickles soaking in their own juice. The bread and cheese seemed to have lost all vestiges of moisture, and the bologna had curled up at the edges. "Deuces are wild," Dave was saying, "and so are one-eyed jacks. At least for this hand."

Molly nodded numbly. This whole scene was all too familiar. She had lived through it every Saturday night for the three years of her marriage to Steve. The weekly poker game. The stale beer and smelly cigars. The off-color jokes. The man talk: *Honey, get us another six-pack from the refrigerator, would you?* She would sit in the kitchen, leafing through a magazine or working on some needlepoint while "the boys" played poker in the living room. She was privy to their world only through the little snatches of conversation and cigar smoke that drifted into the kitchen. Each time she would carry in another six-pack, she'd be told what a

145

great little wife she was. And then she would hurry back to the kitchen as quickly as she could disengage Steve's hand from her behind.

Seeing Sean so at ease in this setting made her heart sink. She didn't want any part in these macho rituals. Let the boys play out their games without Molly Carter. She'd had enough machismo to last a lifetime.

As though he'd read her mind, Sean touched her left hand, which was balled into a tight fist on the edge of her chair. Gently, he uncurled her fingers and laced them with his own. She glanced at him and then quickly back to the cards in her right hand. His fingers played over her knuckles. "It takes a nickel to open, honey," he said, giving her hand a last squeeze before withdrawing his fingers. "You can use my nickels." He pointed to the pile between them.

"Hardly seems fair, making Molly bet with money when she's never played poker before," Breck said, rubbing his chin thoughtfully. "Couldn't she use something else?"

"Matches?" Rod suggested.

"Toothpicks?" Dave added.

Sean shook his head. "I've got just the thing." He stood up and went to the kitchen, returning a moment later with a plastic bag

146

that he plopped down in front of Molly. "There you go, ma'am," he said with a grin. "Your own bag of marshmallows."

Molly felt a smile tugging at the corners of her mouth as the others laughed out loud. "All right!" Breck whooped. "Now that's something worth gambling for."

The game opened and Molly tried to concentrate. The sooner she got through all this, the better. She laid two cards face down and Dave dealt her two new ones, but Rod shook his head and told Dave to give her another card. "Discard that five," Rod advised her. "And hold your cards up higher," he added with a grin.

Molly nodded ruefully. They all broke into laughter when the nickels were tossed in the center of the table and Molly's marshmallow followed.

Beer tabs popped and the lunchmeat plate made the rounds again. Sean lit up a cigar and grinned at her, one eye squinting against the smoke. "They're foul things, I know," he said, "but I only smoke when I play poker."

"Thank heavens," Molly couldn't help saying.

One beer and half a slice of cheese later, Molly was beginning to relax. Poker wasn't so tough to learn after all. Her hours of playing bridge with her family had at least taught her to keep track of which cards had been played. Soon she had a pretty good idea of what hands were most likely to take the pot.

"I'll see your nickel," Molly said, raising her eyebrows, "and raise you two marshmallows."

"Whoa, man!" Rod cried. "I don't know if I can cover two marshmallows."

"This is getting too rich for my blood," Dave said with a shake of his head.

Molly won the hand, and Rod clapped her on the back and opened another can of beer for her. Molly found herself grinning at the faces around the table and laughing a second later when Rod began munching on the marshmallows in the pot.

"Thoreau should be here," Sean remarked. "I bet he could stuff those marshmallows in with both paws."

"Thoreau?" Dave repeated.

Sean told them about the raccoon he'd rescued and Molly's choice of name for the creature.

"Wise woman," Rod said, nodding as he dealt a new hand. "I'm a fan of old Henry David myself."

"You?" Molly couldn't hide the surprise in her voice.

"Sure." Rod flicked a potato chip from his flight jacket. "When I got out of high school I built a cabin in the woods and vowed to live there off the land. I read Thoreau by candlelight at night and planted a vegetable garden by day. I lasted all of two months."

"What happened?" Molly asked.

"The rabbits overran my garden, the mice overran my cabin, and I froze my a—" He cleared his throat. "I froze my buns off the first hard freeze. It was awful."

"That wasn't what really got to him, though," Breck said with a gleam in his eye. "His mom refused to send him any more chocolate-chip cookies until he got a decent job."

They all broke into loud laughter, and Rod grinned sheepishly. "Those cookies are damn good," he defended himself, provoking still more hilarity.

It was almost eleven when Molly leaned back and surveyed the pile of nickels and marshmallows in front of her. Dave had just told a slightly blue joke about a penguin, and Molly followed it with one about two ministers arriving in heaven.

Laughing and stretching, Dave got to his feet, followed by Breck and Rod. Rod gave Molly an affectionate pat on the shoulder as he passed, and they all trooped out the sliding glass door, breaking into loud song as they made their way to their cars.

Molly stood up unsteadily as the last car pulled away and Sean closed the door. "The big winner," Sean said with a gentle smile as he walked to the table. Molly glanced at the pile of nickels and marshmallows. "I hereby donate my winnings to the refreshment fund for the next poker game," she intoned. "That bologna and cheese was really the pits."

Sean nodded. "I forgot about the game until I got home tonight, and I didn't have anything in the house." His eyes sought out hers. "I guess I had other things on my mind."

Molly's gaze slid to the table. There had been many things on her mind too since the last time she'd seen Sean.

She slowly walked to the other side of the table, a whimsical smile flitting across her face as she righted one of the empty beer cans and brushed a finger over the stray marshmallow lying beside it.

"I'm glad you came," Sean said, watching her.

She gave a half-nod, tracing a pattern on the table. Restlessly she toyed with the bow at her throat. "It was fun," she said.

Sean sighed and ran a hand through his

hair. "You didn't expect to have fun when you walked in here, did you?"

Molly raised her head to look at him. The green eyes caught hers and held them. "It wasn't what I thought it would be," she admitted.

"And what did you think it would be?" he demanded.

"It was a poker game," Molly said defensively. "Four guys, a lot of beer, cigars. I expected it to be like . . ." Her voice trailed off.

"Like Steve's poker games?" Sean asked.

Molly nodded. "They looked like the usual group of macho guys, Sean. For heaven's sake, Rod was wearing a flight jacket."

"How much more macho can you get?" Sean said derisively. "Molly, don't you see what you did when you walked in here? You took one look and thought, *Oh, my God, this is just like Steve*. A flight jacket does not make a man's man. Just like the right coloring does not make a pipe-vine swallowtail. Don't you understand that yet?"

She stared back at him, the energy draining out of her as his eyes pierced her shell. "You're right," she said wearily, pressing her fingertips to her forehead. "I walked in here, took one look, and all the old stereotypes glittered in front of my eyes like a neon sign. I'm sorry. I had a good time tonight, and I really liked your friends."

"They liked you too. You're a pretty great lady, Molly." He walked to her slowly and put his arms around her waist.

"Sean." She stiffened in his embrace, and he drew back far enough to look into her face. "I don't think I'm so great," she murmured in a tight voice, pressing her fists to her eyes.

"Why not?"

"I made so many mistakes with Steve," she said almost in a whisper. "I couldn't seem to get the marriage to work. It was like there was some kind of bridge between us, but it didn't meet in the middle, and the gap was too far to leap across." She shook her head wearily. "Maybe I just didn't try hard enough. I never asked him if I could sit in on his poker games. I didn't want to see him trying to prove his masculinity over and over, so I never went to watch him race cars or motorcycles or boats." The tears were beginning to escape from the corners of her eyes and trickle down her cheeks, and she swiped at them with her palms. "I didn't even go with him the night he crashed. And he died." Her voice cracked and the tears poured out in an unstoppable torrent. Sean pressed her head to his chest and stroked her hair, holding her tightly against him.

Her own arms closed around his waist, and she clung to him unsteadily.

Sean half carried her to the couch and sat down, Molly cradled on his lap. Her palms moved up to press his shoulder blades, and her sobs gradually quieted. He stroked her hair with one hand, his other gently massaging the back of her neck. "Let it go, Molly," he whispered soothingly. "Let the pain go."

She felt completely drained, as though the last six years of her life had just run through her soul and poured out her throat, carrying with them all the pain and bitterness that had built up during her three-year marriage and its lonely aftermath. She rested her head against Sean's chest, hearing the reassuring heartbeat and feeling the warmth of his body. Molly Carter had come in from the cold after a long fight, and she allowed herself finally to take comfort in the presence of another human being. She had always felt like an interloper before, a stranger entering the homes of others just long enough to warm herself slightly at their fire before she left to face the cold alone again.

Molly was loath to let go of him, and she held on to the curl of heat growing inside her as Sean gently rocked her. His hand smoothed down her hair and gentled her neck and caressed her back. Molly pressed herself more tightly against him, bemused by her own acknowledgment of need. Sean's finger curved around the collar of her blouse and lifted her chin carefully. She dragged her blue eyes open and met his searching green ones. He seemed satisfied with what he saw, and a gentle smile touched his mouth. She shifted slightly in his embrace, and his finger traced the bow at her throat, trailing down quite naturally to the buttons of her silk blouse and then to the swelling fullness of her breast.

He caressed it in ever smaller circles until he cupped his palm over its fullness. Molly arched her body against him, wanting to feel his strength through her blouse, through her skirt, and against her bare flesh. His mouth sought and found hers, brushing her lips lightly until she parted them hungrily. He claimed her then with every weapon in his seductive arsenal. Sensitive fingers fondled her breasts while his mouth covered hers in heart-stopping possessiveness.

Her hands kneaded the flesh over his shoulder blades, urgently stroking up and down, reveling in the play of muscle beneath her hands. One hand curved upward to his head, and her fingers toyed with the thick, silky hair. She breathed his name against his mouth, answering him kiss for kiss as his lips became more compelling.

He broke away while she was still straining toward him, and a long moment passed before she opened glazed eyes to stare at him curiously. He still bore a faint flush high on his cheekbones, and his eyes burned with a fiery green light. She reached up slowly to cup his cheek in her palm, but he caught her hand and brought it to his mouth, brushing it with his lips. She wanted to stay with him tonight, to take what strength she could from him. He was a fortress against her loneliness, and she needed him badly. Molly had always worn her independence like a talisman, and this feeling of need was new and frightening. She wanted to explore it with Sean.

Just let me lay my head on your pillow, cradle your body to mine. Just let me be with you tonight.

Slowly he shook his head, as if he'd read her mind. "Not tonight," he whispered. "I don't want to make love to you when you're feeling this way. You're still hurting, love."

He helped her to her feet and held her against his body. She felt a heavy sigh run through him. "Come on," he said softly. "I'll drive you home."

Through the haze of sweet languor pulsing through her, she saw the moon riding high above the trees outside his house and the starkly shadowed pines lining the ridges like sentries. "I can drive myself," she said quietly, resting her head on his shoulder as they walked out the door toward the car. "I'm all right."

"Are you sure?"

She nodded, extricating herself from his arm and staring up at the sky. Her gaze fell on the twinkling stars of Capricorn. Swiftly she swung her eyes back to her car. "Good night," she said.

"Good night," he echoed softly, his hand trailing through her hair as he held the door open for her. "Sleep well, Molly."

All the way home she carried the memory of his face like a golden treasure.

Chapter 7

Molly balanced Thoreau on one arm and pulled a cheese cracker from a bag with her free hand. Three children watched in rapt attention as she handed the cracker to Thoreau and he inspected it carefully before holding it up to his mouth, his dark eyes bright.

The mall would close in fifteen minutes, and the crowd was thinning out. The Forest Service exhibit had done a brisk business all day, thanks in no small part to Thoreau. This was Outdoor Weekend, so proclaimed by the mall merchants, mostly to push sales of camping and recreation equipment. The booths sat in an ordered row down the middle aisle of the mall. A local boat shop had set up its exhibit next to the Forest Service table, and the owner, a young businessman type in a three-piece suit, had leaned on Molly's table and announced that he'd bring a live moose next year to outdraw her raccoon. He had brushed back his too-neatly layered hair, whisked a fleck of imaginary lint from his moustache, and asked her to join him for some wine after the mall closed. Molly had politely declined.

Now she felt a sudden quickening of her pulse and looked up to see Sean leaning in the doorway to the bookstore, lazily observing her and the kids. In one glance she took in the slim jeans-clad hips and firm torso covered by a chambray shirt and wheat-colored fisherman's sweater. He had the damnedest habit of always looking terrific, no matter what he wore. She knew he was deliberately holding back where she was concerned, downplaying the sexual chemistry between them out of concern for her mixed emotions. But that knowledge had done nothing to relieve the ache last night when she lay alone in her bed wishing he'd invited her to spend the night with him. Somehow that made her feel a little awkward around him today.

Molly put Thoreau back in his cage and showed the kids a glass display case with leaf samples. "Chlorophyll makes a leaf green," Molly explained, smiling at the three intent faces, a little boy of about ten and his two younger sisters, all blond. Three sets of small fingers gripped the edge of the table tightly. "In the fall the chlorophyll fades," Molly went on, "and the other colors that were there all the time become visible. A dogwood leaf will turn red, and a poplar leaf yellow. Now, do any of you know what makes a leaf fall from the tree?"

One of the girls looked up at Molly solemnly. "My daddy says the devil makes leaves fall. Just so he has to rake them."

Molly hid her smile. "There's another reason," she said. "When the leaves turn colors, a special layer forms between the leaf and its branch. It's like cork, and it's called the absciss layer. It's very weak, so any little gust of wind can break it and make the leaf fall. Some trees don't form this layer, and they carry their leaves late into winter. Do you know any trees like that?"

Three blond heads shook in unison.

Molly pointed to two pictures in the case. "Oak and beech. These two here."

"Billy," a woman called as she hurried toward them with an armload of packages. "Get your sisters and let's go back to the car. The mall's closing."

"Mom," Billy shouted in excitement as he ran toward her. "Did you know that raccoons eat cheese crackers and oak trees don't have ab . . . absisters? Where do raccoons get cheese crackers in the woods, Mom?" Billy's two sisters ran after their brother spilling out other tidbits of information, albeit in slightly

159

altered fashion. "Leaves have choloroform, Mommy," one of the little girls was explaining importantly as they walked toward the doors. Molly leaned back and watched them with a wistful smile. They might not have all the facts straight, but something of her talk would stay with them, and maybe when they were older that something would spark a serious interest in the world of nature.

She bent down and began packing pamphlets and photographs into boxes. She could hear an iron gate sliding over the entrance to the bookstore. When she stood up, she found herself staring at a wheat-colored chest right in front of her table. Slowly she raised her eyes.

His head was cocked to one side, his eyes alive with amusement. "Why do forest rangers have such curvy hips, Mommy?" he murmured softly.

"Because they have chloroform in their blood," she answered lightly. She cast a quick glance around the mall. "Now if Gil would just show up, I could move these things out of here."

"Gil's not coming," Sean said, easily pushing aside a long folding table and joining her inside the display. "Here, I'll do that." He pried her fingers from the display case and hefted it into a box on the floor.

"What do you mean Gil's not coming?" she demanded.

"I volunteered to pick you up, along with your display. I think he wanted to go into town tonight anyway."

"And you had nothing better to do tonight," she retorted, slightly irritated by his casual interference with her plans.

"Let's not get out of sorts," he said soothingly. "I fully intend to deliver you and your pamphlets safely to your doorstep." He gestured at the exhibit and stopped abruptly. "By the way, where's Thoreau?"

"He's in his —" She broke off in horror when she saw the open door on the empty cage. "Oh, Lord! The monster's on the loose. The mall's going to sue the Forest Service."

Her worst fears were confirmed as she heard a sudden scream from the vicinity of the expensive department store whose entrance was only a few feet from her exhibit. She and Sean broke for the store at the same instant, but Sean got a head start by leaping over the exhibit table.

The perfume counter was just inside the door, and a dignified-looking woman with salt and pepper hair was standing there like a statue, her hand clapped over her mouth, her eyes wide behind large round glasses. When she saw Sean and Molly, she pointed to her right. Molly raced after Sean, moaning when she glanced back over her shoulder and saw the overturned bottles of perfume on the counter, like so many bowling pins on an alley.

The next scream came from the lingerie department, and Sean gamely trooped into the bra section, followed by a frantic Molly. "He was running along the camisoles," the young clerk said, disbelief in her voice. "What is he — a rat?"

"Only in the figurative sense," Molly retorted. Molly and Sean crept warily down the aisle, bras mounted on either side of them on dummies' torsos. "Looks like a damn trophy room," Sean muttered. "You don't see men's shorts displayed like stuffed game animals on a wall."

"Men's shorts don't come in five hundred styles and colors," Molly said shortly. "There he is!"

Thoreau was just disappearing into a sea of underwear on a sale table two aisles over, looking like a furry little burglar awash in pastel satins. Molly gave chase and banged into a rack of gauzy nightgowns along the way. The clatter of plastic hangers hitting one another startled Thoreau, and he was off again in a flash of lavender and lace, dragging a filmy wisp of lingerie after him.

They finally caught up with him at Popalong Cassidy's, the popcorn shop across the way. Thoreau was perched on the top display shelf, enthusiastically ripping open a cellophane-wrapped can of caramel corn, a sheer, beribboned, corset-style camisole in pale lavender dangling from his rear paw.

Sean stepped up to the counter where the young clerk was staring at the display in stunned disbelief. "I think we'll take that can of caramel corn," Sean said matter-of-factly, nodding toward the top shelf, "and a bag of that purple stuff over there."

Sean laid several dollar bills on the counter, then calmly reached up and retrieved Thoreau and his can of caramel corn. He smiled at the clerk and started out the door, Molly following behind with visions of lawsuits dancing in her head.

As they were loading the exhibit into Sean's truck, Molly double-checked the lock on Thoreau's cage. "I don't think the Forest Service will ever be welcome in that mall again," she muttered.

Sean held up the lavender camisole he'd purchased to extricate Molly and Thoreau from a threatened legal action by the department store. "The evening wasn't a total loss," he reminded her, grinning wickedly.

"It's too small for me," Molly hastily assured him.

Sean scrutinized the garment. "These ribbons are adjustable," he observed. "I think it'll do just fine."

His finger lingered on the ecru lace edging the bodice, and Molly turned away as her heart lurched. The pulse in her throat was throbbing uncontrollably. She climbed into the front of the truck and waited while he closed the tailgate and came around to the driver's side.

He dropped the lacy garment in her lap and gave her a crooked smile as he started the engine, and Molly sat primly with her hands folded over the camisole all the way back to the ranger station. Her heart was beating wildly, and she felt powerless to slow it down. Some barrier had fallen last night while she'd cried in his arms, and Sean's effect on her was more intoxicating than ever. She couldn't stop remembering how his fingers had weaved their spell up and down her spine and in all sorts of other intimate places. As the truck pulled up in front of the ranger station, Molly realized she was fingering the lace of the camisole dreamily. Abruptly she jumped down from the truck and began helping Sean unload the exhibit. He released the tailgate and they both reached for the same box at the same time. His fingers felt like fire on her own, and he quickly took her hand in his, massaging it. "You're cold as ice," he said. "Get inside, and I'll unload."

No words could make their way past the constriction in her throat, so she nodded hastily and headed straight for the door as soon as he released her hand.

She had just set two cups of hot tea on the table when he entered the kitchen. He seemed to fill the entire doorway. "I put everything in your office," he said, his eyes coming to rest on the camisole she'd laid on the counter.

"I made some tea," she said quickly. "Are you hungry? I've got a little coffee cake."

"Sounds good." He sat down at the table and put a bag of purple popcorn by her cup. "I don't know what flavor this is, but it looks interesting."

"Never, but never," she said wryly, "tell a clerk that you'll take a bag of the purple stuff. It could be eggplant flavored for all we know."

Sean grinned. "When you're dealing with a wayward raccoon, rules don't apply. Besides, if it's eggplant we'll make Thoreau eat it."

She set the coffee cake on the table with two plates and sat down, cutting the cake to keep her hands busy. Rules didn't always apply in other situations either, she thought to herself. She was discovering that there were very few rules where Sean was concerned.

They ate in silence, and Molly's eyes kept drifting to the camisole she'd tossed on the counter. She sensed an undercurrent between her and Sean tonight, a rawness to their emotions.

He tasted some of the purple popcorn after they'd cleared the dishes. "Mmm, grape."

Molly made a face. "Grape popcorn is symptomatic of our society. Plain old buttered isn't good enough anymore. We have to have a new thrill every day or life isn't exciting enough."

"Another opinion worthy of Henry David Thoreau and Walden Pond," Sean said approvingly, but she caught the hint of amusement in his voice.

She stood up from the table abruptly and carried her cup and saucer to the sink. They clattered together loudly when she set them down. "Maybe I should just go off into the forest and build myself a cabin like Thoreau did," she said, half in jest. "Then I wouldn't be assailed by things like grape popcorn and department stores that look unkindly on raccoons." She ran water in the sink, stiffening when she heard Sean come up behind her.

His hand stroked the slender column of her neck, his thumb trailing up and down the nape. "Molly," he murmured, gently but firmly turning her face to him. His hand slid up to capture her chin, his finger rubbing softly along her jaw. "Rod tried that and it didn't work," he said. "It wasn't just his mother's cookies and his frozen rear end that brought him back to civilization. He told me once that while he lived in that cabin he was accountable to no one, and he hated every minute of it. Human beings aren't meant to live alone, Molly. When they're committed to nothing more than themselves, there's no real purpose to their lives." His eyes were the deep green of the forest's inner recesses and staring into them she saw a fire that ignited her soul.

He brought his mouth down on hers, hard, and Molly resolved she wouldn't beggar away any more pieces of her life to Sean, not when she could no longer control that life. She felt her insides unraveling like a skein of metallic yarn, and she couldn't stop it. Sean's mouth was the only thing that made sense at this crazy moment in her kitchen, and she responded to it fully. Her palm claimed the back of his neck, stroking fervently, while her fingers tangled in his hair.

Sean moved one hand behind her, sliding it down her hip and cupping her bottom to bring her body close against his. His muscled thighs dragged against her trembling legs, making her aware as no words could that he was deepening the demands he would make of her. His lips moved tortuously down her neck until his head rested heavily at her shoulder.

"Molly," he groaned. Her fingers tightened in his hair, and he shivered. "You know what I want, Molly. You've been running away from it like a skittish colt. You won't let yourself trust me. You won't let us have what you couldn't have with Steve. Don't deny yourself again."

"I'm not running away," she said in a low voice, still reeling from his touch. "You're the one who chased me out of your house last night, Sean."

"Before I chased you out you'd already walked away from me emotionally. You say you want an isolated cabin, Molly — well, you've built one inside yourself and you lock the door when I get too close. What hap-

168

pened between you and Steve is over. Let yourself go, Molly. Quit hiding from me."

She shook her head wordlessly, waiting for the lump in her throat to dissolve so she could speak. "I don't know what you want," she said helplessly.

"I want you to trust me. To at least think about the possibility of a future between us."

"I do," she protested.

His fingers gripped her shoulders tightly. "Then why the hell didn't you tell me about the staff position in Asheville? Didn't you think that had any bearing on our future?"

Her eyes flew open, dismay evident. She felt as though he had taken one step closer to that part of her she was so determined to keep from him. "How did you find out?" she demanded.

"Gil told me." He shook his head. "I'm here for you, Molly. Can't you understand that?"

"I'm sorry. I didn't think to tell you."

"Look at me." His voice was low. "I gave you ample opportunity to tell me what was on your mind last night. You made a conscious choice not to tell me, Molly. Don't pretend otherwise."

His hands fell from her shoulders, and he took a step backward. She braced herself mentally, recognizing the resolve in his face. "I can't compete with your idealized Mr. Thoreau," he said coolly. "When you get tired of waiting for him to appear, you know where to find me." He stood there watching her for another moment, and Molly tried desperately to say something that would keep him from going. But she couldn't force the words out, and he slowly turned and walked away from her.

She wandered around the kitchen aimlessly, wiping already clean counters with a dishrag. She knew she wasn't waiting for an idealized vision to step out of the woods anymore. Sean had already done that. But Sean on his own terms meant total commitment. And the price was too high. Because Molly knew instinctively that she would come to love Sean Feyer far more deeply than she'd ever loved Steve. The pain and anger she'd suffered over Steve would be nothing compared to the devastation of loving Sean and losing him.

The loggers moved into the forest on Monday, Sean with them, and Molly watched stolidly as the jeeps ferried men in hard hats, gloves, and work boots up the timber road. She stood beside her own jeep talking to the foreman, a walking muscle of a man with thick white hair and bright blue eyes sunk into a weathered face that was sharply seamed by endless hours in the sun.

Leif Thornton stood with his hamhock arms crossed over his barrel chest as the jeeps passed by. "Looks like we're all set to start cutting," he barked out. "You all ready, hon?" Molly nodded and climbed into the jeep with Leif. He called his men "bub" and "pal," and she figured "hon" was preferable to either of those. They fell into line behind one of the huge Cats crawling up the road after the jeeps, and Leif shouted above the noise, "You got an assistant to do the scaling?"

"Gil Peterson. He's already at the site."

Molly got out with Leif at the first stand of trees marked for cutting and made a quick scan of the lumberjacks' faces. Her eyes came to rest on a pair of green eyes watching her from the shadows of a large pine. Sean was dressed like the others, in a hard hat, flannel shirt, work jeans, and sturdy boots. He was leaning against the tree, his mouth a straight line that betrayed no emotion, and she swallowed. She wondered if he felt the same charged excitement rippling through his veins that she did. Just the sight of him stirred her flesh to heated response. His eyes seemed to play down her neck, and she could almost feel his touch. This was going to be harder than she'd imagined.

She turned away as Leif called to his men, and the cutters picked up their chainsaws and began fanning out through the trees. Molly watched the easy movement of Sean's long legs and slim hips as he blended into the forest. He was such a beautiful man.

Molly's job was to work closely with the timber crew, and she was determined to maintain a professional attitude despite Sean's distracting presence. Using her ax, she helped clear underbrush around the marked trees and guided the cutters through the surveyed area.

A cry of "down the road" rang through the trees, and Molly stood back to watch in awe as a large pine came crashing down. It bounced once, then came to rest on the needle floor like a felled giant. Molly moved in to trim away the smaller branches from the main trunk, and stepped directly into the path of a man behind her. He caught her arm to keep from knocking her over, and she hurriedly began to apologize. But when she looked over her shoulder, her voice died in her throat. It was Sean touching her. She should have known. Wildfire had seared through her shirt like a branding iron even before she knew it was his hand. His fingers moved just enough, pressed just enough, to make the touch intimate rather than casual. She mentally cursed him. Was he immune to the electricity between them? His hand slid down her arm to her hand.

"Could I borrow your ax a minute?" he asked politely, and she could read no emotion in his eyes. Angered, she handed him the ax and quickly turned away. She watched him work on the tree from beneath the overhanging branches of a rhododendron, absently rubbing the arm he'd touched. She could still feel the imprint of his fingers on her, and she was sure that if she rolled up her sleeve the flesh would be flushed and warm. Worse than that, tentacles of pleasure had spread from her shoulder and arm and threatened to undermine her very sanity. The timber cutting would take weeks. She'd never make it . . .

Morning swelled into noon, and cold white autumn sun highlighted the stark, leafless trees. The forest floor glowed like crystal. Molly sat down on a stump next to Leif and two other men and unwrapped her lunch. She flinched when a long shadow fell across her, and she looked up into a chiseled face sliced into dark and light by the sun. "The Cat's got some trouble," Sean said to Leif, running a hand through his hair. The sun caught it and threw out a thousand gold reflections like the pyrite winking away on Molly's end table at the forest station. "I think it's serious, and it's going to slow us down till we get it fixed. Oil leak."

Leif nodded wearily. "Okay. I'll look at it after lunch. Here, sit down, Sean."

Molly stared at Leif in surprise. Sean was the first man she'd heard Leif address by his real name all morning. She didn't pursue that thought as Sean sank down on the ground beside her, close enough to disturb her breathing, and pulled a sandwich from his lunch pail.

He took a nonchalant bite and leaned back against a tree. "How's Frank doing?" Sean asked, and Molly watched in fascination as Leif nodded and grinned proudly. "Not bad, Sean. Not too bad. Going to make me a grandpa for the second time next year. Hell, I'm feeling as old as the mountains now." He washed down a big bite of sandwich with a swallow from a soda can and flashed a toothy grin. "Won't be long before I'll be turning the logging operation over to the young ones."

Sean shook his head. "You're too mean to quit, Leif. You can cut trees just by looking at them."

Leif chuckled. "I figure I been mellowing

like old wine. Now my little baby grand-daughter calls me Paw-Paw. And hell, I love it."

Sean grinned at him. "My brother's baby girl has Dad wrapped around her little finger too."

Leif suddenly sobered. "I still say a prayer every day, thanking the good Lord I still got Frank. If it weren't for you, he'd've been gone in that fire."

"That's all in the past, Leif," Sean said quietly.

Leif nodded slowly. "Yeah, but if you hadn't been up there in that plane that day . . ." His voice trailed off, and the silence was broken only by the shrill call of a blue jay. It came to Molly that Leif's son Frank must have been the young man in the tractor that Sean had saved when he crashed. Her own eyes grew dark and sober, and she stared off at the trees, not wanting to think about Sean crashing.

"Cockleburrs on everything," Sean muttered, and Molly's attention was abruptly jerked back to him as she felt his hand on her calf. She jumped and swung her eyes to him beside her. He seemed intent on the burrs stuck to her uniform leg, pulling them off one by one. But his hand lingered longer each time he touched her, and Molly could

175

barely swallow her sandwich. As he pulled a burr from the hem of her pants leg, his fingers brushed her ankle delicately and Molly had to stifle a sudden groan. His fingers roamed gently upward beneath her hem, and her flesh ached for more. But with a satisfied grunt he tossed away the burr and went back to his sandwich. Molly forced herself to swallow, then resolutely got to her feet. "I guess I'd better check on Gil," she murmured weakly, tossing her unfinished sandwich back into her lunch bag. Her appetite had fled — her appetite for food, that is. At the moment, however, she was starved for Sean's touch. She walked toward the jeep, not really seeing anything. Weeks of this tantalizing hunger stretched ahead of her. Weeks of Sean's impersonal presence and cool gaze. Weeks of his casual touch. Weeks? One more day like this and she'd be dead of frustration.

Tuesday Molly was walking toward a clearing when Sean suddenly stepped in front of her and she plowed right into him. He caught her in his arms with a politely murmured, "Are you okay?" and held on just long enough to start her blood boiling. She was breathing with difficulty and she knew her skin was flushed by the time he released her and strode away. She couldn't sleep that night for the erotic dreams.

Wednesday he sat down between her and Leif at lunchtime and spent the half-hour carrying on a mundane conversation with the logging foreman while his leg idly brushed Molly's. She spent that afternoon muttering darkly to the trees.

Thursday she managed to avoid him all day and was just congratulating herself on her emotional survival when he came up behind her. She was leaning against a pine tree, her hard hat in her hand. "You really should wear this all the time," he said solicitously, taking the hat from her nerveless fingers. His voice sent shivers down her spine. He stepped in front of her and made a production of placing the hat on her head, managing to tangle his hands in her hair and trail them down her face to her neck in the process. "A little dirt on your collar," he explained gravely as he brushed at her throat. Molly swayed unsteadily. She could have sworn there'd been a fiery glitter in his eyes a moment ago, but now it was gone, and Sean nodded crisply before walking away.

When Molly got home that night she found the simplest task, like fixing dinner, beyond her abilities. She had completely breaded the chicken before she remembered she was supposed to debone and skin it first. She gave Thoreau a banana to keep him occupied and began peeling a carrot. She had already shaved it down to a nub by the time she finally glanced down and saw what she was doing.

She couldn't stop thinking about Sean and the shivers of pleasure that rippled through her every time he connived to touch her in the course of their work together. Saying no to him was like telling a hurricane, *Thanks, but I don't need any rain today* — an exercise in futility. She leaned against the sink and rubbed her forehead. Somewhere along the line her "no" had become a "yes." She just hadn't admitted it. She had held back from Sean out of habit, a long-practiced mode of self-preservation. Self-preservation had taken on new meanings with Sean. She suddenly realized that if she continued trying to hold him at arm's length, something vital inside her would begin cracking and crumbling until she was only a hollow shell.

Molly looked at Thoreau chewing the banana and smiled. The fur was beginning to grow back where he had been burned, and he looked like a teenager out of the 1950s with a flattop haircut. He had regained almost normal mobility with his rear paw.

Soon she would have to set him free. The vision of him contentedly eating the banana was somewhat illusory. He was a wild animal, after all, and he belonged in the forest.

It was the same with her own defensive shell. That, too, was just an illusion. Sean thought it impenetrable, but he had already reached her deep inside — even if he didn't realize it.

She dropped the chicken cutlet on the hot iron skillet and watched the bubbles of moisture hiss and spin. Whatever happened between her and Sean, she was going to meet it head on. No more illusion.

Chapter 8

Once again Molly found sleep was elusive. She sat at the living-room window wrapped in a comforter, idly stroking Thoreau, who was intently playing with a loose thread from the lace collar of her robe. Night shrouded the mountain like a thick curtain, hiding even the stars from view. Molly stared through the cold glass, trying to pick out the dark shapes of trees beyond the porch. She reached for the cup of hot cocoa on the end table and her fingers encountered the pyrite instead. Sparks of electric desire danced up her arms, radiating from the pyrite. It took only a memory of Sean these days to ignite this devouring longing. It invaded her waking hours as well as her dreams. Abruptly she withdrew her hand from the rock.

A pinpoint of light flashed in the distance, down the gravel road, and Molly pressed her forehead against the glass, murmuring to Thoreau. The light separated and became twin headlights and Molly drew back from the curtain as the beams swung over the station and the pickup truck drew to a stop outside.

She leaned closer as the truck's door opened and Sean stepped out, standing stock still to stare at the station. Molly's breath made foggy patches on the window-pane, but she didn't move. Although there was no way he could possibly see her, she was unable to rid herself of the ridiculous notion that with Sean she somehow became crystal to his olivine eyes.

His footsteps thudded on the porch and then there was silence. She hardly dared breathe, much less move. An eternity later the truck door opened and closed. She heard the engine start, its low whine slowly fading into the dark. The first apricot-tinged breath of sunrise hazed the mountains.

She sat still a while longer and then gripped her comforter tightly and went to the door. A whisper of chill air breached her wrap at the ankles and she shivered. In front of the door was a brown bag. After a hasty look around, Molly brought it inside.

She went back to the rocking chair by the window and watched Thoreau cleaning his whiskers on the sill. Sean's shadowy image was burned on her mind, and it was several minutes before she glanced back down at the bag. She carefully unfolded the top and peered inside. She pulled out a bottle of wine and squinted as she tried to read the label. All she could make out was something French.

There was more in the bag from the weight, and she poked her hand back in. What the . . . ? Nuts? She caught one of the smooth round objects and held it in front of her face. A chestnut. She took the bag. Lots of chestnuts.

She set the bag on the floor and stood up restlessly. Without thinking, she moved to the end table and picked up the pyrite. As she stroked it absently with her thumb, she thought about the swallowtail butterflies in their cocoons for the winter, a metamorphic slumber changing their shapes. Sighing, she set down the pyrite and ran her hands down her sides, slowly touching her hips, almost as if she expected to find her own body changed. Some metamorphoses occurred on the inside, she suddenly realized. And if you tried to stop them halfway, before they were complete, then you'd just hang there like a butterfly in its cocoon. And in that moment, Molly made a decision: she was going to talk it out with Sean today.

Molly watched Sean grimly. He'd avoided

her all day, his eyes like opaque glass the one time they met hers. He hadn't touched her once. Now it was quitting time, and she stood watching him from the shadow of a tree.

The chainsaw split the air with its droning screech, its teeth spitting wood chips from the undercut Sean had started. When the wedge-shaped chunk of wood had been cut out, he stopped the chainsaw and wiped his forehead with the back of his hand. His red plaid flannel shirt was rolled up to the elbows despite the chill air, and the muscles of his forearms were knotted with the weight of the saw. His thighs pressed the worn fabric of his jeans as he moved to the opposite side of the tree. She watched him run a critical eye over the trunk and then gaze at the area beyond the tree where a small clearing spread out in the waning sun. He moved to the tree and started the saw again, making a backcut in the wood. Perspiration beaded his face and arms. He stopped the saw long enough to use a sledgehammer to drive a metal wedge into the backcut to keep the tree from pinching the saw. Then the saw was whining again, Sean's back muscles rock-hard under the straining flannel. The saw's teeth bit deeply into the tree trunk, and more shavings flew as the clean white wood was exposed. Sean glanced up once at the top of the tree and momentarily raised his head. "Down the road!" he hollered, drawing out the words like song lyrics. A loud crack drowned out the chainsaw, and Sean jerked it away from the tree, stepping back out of the way. The massive tree trembled like a matchstick balanced upright on a finger, and then it toppled.

A thundering giant, the tree crashed into the clearing, limbs and leaves rustling and snapping beneath its weight. An awesome silence reigned in the forest for a long moment before a squirrel resumed its chatter from the height of a pine, and a bird called shrilly in the distance. Molly watched Sean's eyes gleam with male satisfaction. The tree had hit the bull's-eye in loggers' parlance. It had fallen exactly where Sean planned.

"Very nice," she said, stepping out of the shadows.

He laid down the saw and slowly pulled off his work gloves. He took two steps toward her, out of the forest darkness and into a shaft of lavender light from the setting sun. The ever-present smoke gathered in the treetops and boiled in from the mountainside. It drifted around them like wisps of silk, muting the sun's last rays.

"You make swift, clean cuts when you

work," she said quietly. "Too bad you don't sever relationships as smoothly."

He crossed his arms and watched her, his eyes growing stormy though his face didn't alter. "I wasn't trying to sever our relationship," he began with deadly calm. "I just wanted to hear one rational reason why you couldn't tell me about the Asheville position. Why you couldn't trust me enough to open up a little."

"I'm not used to opening up," she said angrily. "Old habits die hard. I didn't want to dump on you."

A bird flew overhead and settled in the treetop with a rustling of wings, and then the forest was silent again. Sean's voice was derisive. "Dump on me?" he echoed. "That wasn't the point, Molly, and you know it. There's a part of yourself that you're determined to keep untouchable. I just can't live with that."

"And your solution was to give me that stupid exit line," she snapped, her voice rising. She took another step toward him, her hands on her hips. "*If you get tired of waiting for your Thoreau to walk out of the forest, you know where to find me.* Something like that, wasn't it, Sean? Now, what the hell kind of thing was that to say?"

"I had to do something to drum it

through your thick head that we belong together," he growled, matching her stance, lean fingers hooked in his belt. "I thought that might shake you up enough so you'd take a good hard look at what we could have together." His jaw clenched, and green fire leaped into his eyes. "Dammit, Molly, I wanted you to miss me." The plaintive note in his voice tugged at her heart and she suddenly found herself remembering the night they'd danced together under the moon and stars.

Was it the smoke rolling in that made everything so ghostly, or was it the mist in her eyes?

"How could I miss you?" she demanded in frustration, "when I saw you every day and when you contrived to touch me at every opportunity? How could I miss you when you were here all the time, doing your best to drive me crazy?"

His voice was deep and compelling, even as it registered his sharp impatience. "Don't you realize that you can exist side by side with a person and not really be with them?" The words pierced her shell of anger and sparked the embers. "Don't you know that yet, Molly, even after Steve?"

She saw his game now, the teasing, the elusive physical contact, the many small ways he had made her miss him. "Congratulations, Sean," she retorted. "You're absolutely right. My marriage was simply two people existing together. No, not even together. Existing separately. I don't want that again, ever. And you're pushing me to begin something with you that has no guarantees. You're pushing hard, Sean." Her voice had risen two octaves. From the corner of her eye she saw a line of jeeps filled with lumberjacks winding down the timber road, curious heads turned in their direction.

"Yes, I'm pushing you!" He took two strides forward so that he stood just inches away, his eyes blazing down at her. "If I don't push, Molly Carter, you'll be standing in this forest twenty years from now still waiting for your Mr. Thoreau, gilt-edged guarantee in hand, to step up to you and say, 'Here I am. Let's ride off into the sunset.' And, believe me, honey, it'll be a hell of a long wait."

"Dammit, Sean!" she shouted, jerking off her hard hat and throwing it furiously to the ground. "What do you want from me? I can't change overnight. I'm trying, but it's hard. It's very hard." The air between them was still charged with tension, and Molly took a shaky breath, unable to look away from his face.

Her mouth went dry as she watched Sean slowly remove his own hard hat and toss it to the ground beside hers. The gesture was filled with challenge. "Meet me halfway, Molly," he said quietly. "Tell me about yourself — now! You can start with the Asheville job."

She kept her eyes fixed on his face, on those green eyes that sent her pulse leaping and that firm mouth she longed to feel on her own. "Mart Connelson is the district supervisor," she began expressionlessly. "He's moving me to a desk job in Asheville. Apparently I have no choice. I'm to go where I'm sent, and the powers that be are sending me to Asheville."

"Surely you have some kind of choice," he said.

Molly shook her head. "Not really. Field work in the forest is considered a training ground for supervisory positions. I was lucky they allowed me to stay here this long." She jammed her hands in her pockets to hide the fists she'd involuntarily made and lowered her eyes to the ground.

"Maybe I could do something," he suggested.

Molly shook her head. "I doubt it. The forces of bureaucracy keep rolling on. I'll work something out myself." She raised her eyes in time to catch his sharp glance. "By myself," she repeated ruefully. "Well, I did say it was hard to change." Slowly she brought her hands from her pockets and massaged her temples.

"I've never had anyone to turn to, Sean," she explained. "It's a new experience. When my father died, my mom had to farm me out to relatives — until she could make ends meet. I lived in so many homes as a child that I never developed a close relationship with anyone — adult or child, friend or relative. I was a loner from necessity. When you never finish the school year in the same town or celebrate Christmas with the same family, you don't develop any bonds. You said Rod couldn't stand the feeling of being accountable to no one. Well, that's the way I grew up. There wasn't a single person who remained in my life for any length of time. I've been my own family for so long, Sean, that I forget there are other people out there."

"I'm sorry, Molly."

She lowered her hands with a small shrug and watched him step closer to her. "I wish I'd been there when you were a child," he murmured, his eyes moving slowly over her face. "Dammit, Molly. You would have had one person in your life for keeps."

"I know that, Sean." A small smile curved her mouth. "Sometimes that scares me. To think that you're for keeps."

"You better believe it, lady," he murmured huskily. "I want you, Molly. I've wanted you so badly all week that I couldn't think of anything else. You've haunted my dreams and my work in the forest. I couldn't keep my mind — or my hands — off you."

Molly felt her pulse throb at his ardent declaration. The setting sun and the mountain mist had somehow penetrated her skin and were swirling together inside her. The last warmth of the day was singeing her flesh from the inside while the smoke smoldered through her veins, making her feel light-headed and feverish.

"I could tell you about dreams," she murmured, a sigh threading her voice. Her words came out soft and beguiling. "And frustration. But then, what should I expect from a man who leaves a sack of chestnuts and a bottle of wine on my doorstep in the wee hours of the morning?" She lifted her brows and directed a sky-blue gaze at him. "What was *that* all about? And why didn't you knock on the door?" she demanded softly.

His face altered, as though he were imagining what might have transpired if he *had* knocked. The blaze in his eyes smoldered once more. "The wine and chestnuts are an old family tradition. And I was waiting for an invitation," he said, answering both her questions. The timbre of his voice was the wind in the pines. A delicious shiver ran down Molly's spine.

"Consider yourself invited," she whispered. He was only a heartbeat away from her, and she reached out a hand, halting it in mid-air, almost afraid to dispel the magic of the moment. Sean's hand slowly raised and met hers, twining their fingers together. She felt a hot current of desire flash through her body like a bolt of lightning. The swirling smoke seemed charged and alive, capturing them in its gossamer web. She barely felt the damp chill of twilight. Its moisture became the wetness of a kiss.

Sean pulled her to him, and she leaned against his body, her warm breath escaping in a sigh that met and mingled with his groan of possession. She tilted her head up, searching his eyes for the raw desire she knew was there, her blood thickening with hunger for his touch. Sean buried one hand in her hair, his eyes sweeping her face over and over as though memorizing it. He breathed her name as he brought his head down, his lips burning hers, his tongue plunging inside her mouth to touch its sensitive recesses with the sweetness of champagne. The fire that had always existed between them became an inferno, drawing them even closer until her breasts were crushed against his chest and his hard thighs ground into her hips and legs. Lethargy threatened to crumble her trembling knees. She must have staggered or stumbled, because he released her hand to catch her in a devouring embrace.

Her head was bent back and her hand laced tightly around his neck. Her eyes fluttered open briefly, and beyond the silky strands of his hair she could see distant stars in the sky, barely visible through the smoky shroud enveloping them. Sean's mouth never left hers as he slowly lowered Molly to the ground. It flashed through her mind that he was going to make love to her right there in the forest, but she was too lost in passion to protest. The entire timber crew, Gil included, had already gone home. They were alone, and it was dark. Any other considerations were fleeting and soon drowned in the urgency of his desire.

The kiss finally ended, and his hands abandoned her after gently laying her on the ground. Molly reached for him, too bereft to speak, but she was quieted by his husky growl and the warm palm stroking her throat. He was back by her side in an instant, his thick wool jacket in his hand. "Here," he whispered, cradling her to him. "Put this under your back." He nestled her down onto the coat and covered her with his length, propping himself on his elbows. He kissed her again, his large hands cupping her face. Then he straddled his legs on either side of hers, and Molly was vividly reminded of the trench and the feel of his body protectively holding her. Now once more they were locked together in the dark, but this time the fire was raging within them and not above.

Levering himself onto one forearm, Sean watched Molly hungrily as he began to unbutton her shirt with his free hand, fumbling in haste. His hand slipped inside and deftly unhooked the front clip of her bra. The lace was pushed aside, and then he was fondling her breast. She felt her nipple harden as he kneaded the swelling mound, and the fire licking at intimate corners of her body was searing in its intensity. He dragged his fiery green eyes from her crystal blue ones and lowered his head, taking an erect nipple between his lips and swirling his tongue over it. Molly groaned breathlessly and arched against him. His eyes flashed to her again before his mouth lowered to the other breast, and Molly was struck by the hunger she saw in his gaze.

Molly tangled her fingers in his hair, her palm stroking the back of his neck and burrowing under his collar. He pulled himself back up to her throat and pressed his mouth to the pulse throbbing in the hollow. Her hands smoothed down his shirt and made their way to the buttons at the front. Impatiently she pulled at them when she couldn't undo them fast enough. She slid her hand inside and stroked the wiry hair of his chest, then let her fingers trail down to his flat, hard stomach. His intake of breath sweetened her sense of power, and she unbuckled his belt.

Sean rolled to his side, pausing fractionally to brush his hand over her hair and down her cheek. His finger traced a path along her collarbone and throat. Wind moaned through the pines, and ghostly smoke enfolded their entwined bodies. Heat coursed through her, and Molly wondered if this might not be a dream. Each detail of Sean was indelibly etched on her senses, and all sense of time spun down with the smoke.

Sean shrugged out of his shirt and rolled it up into a pillow for Molly's head.

Her hand trembled slightly as she reached up to pull him back down to her. Her palm smoothed the hairs on the back of his neck, and then he was in her arms again, wildly compelling and hungry, the man of her dreams. But this was no dream — it was more real than anything she'd ever experienced in her life.

Sean raised himself to pull off his pants, his eyes raking her face, and Molly could see that he begrudged even those few seconds of time when their bodies weren't touching. And then he was back again and his lips wandered over her throat while his hand caressed her breast. He reached down to her zipper, and she raised her hips when he tugged at her slacks. He feasted his eyes on her, his hand trembling slightly as he stroked her hip. "You're beautiful," he whispered.

"So are you," she murmured with a bemused smile, her eyes caressing the length of his sinewy body. "Are you real, Sean Feyer, or are you some wonderful mirage?"

"I'm real, Molly," he said hoarsely. "As real as these mountains and the pines and the earth under us. I'm no figment of your imagination, and neither is what we're both feeling right now." He pressed himself to her, his pounding heart throbbing against her own. His warmth seemed to permeate her flesh right through to her bones, making her blood boil with the sweetness of his touch.

The musky wool smell of his jacket mingled with the scent of the crushed pine needles beneath them. She ran her hands over his body, loving the infinite variety of textures and planes she encountered, as varied as the shape of the forest. Coarse hair covered his arms, legs, and chest, and on his belly and ribs the skin was silky smooth, a tight covering for the hard, tempered muscles she felt beneath. She arched upward until she could glide her hand over his hip and the uppermost part of his thigh. Sean's head went back, eyes closing as his breath escaped in a ragged sigh.

His thumb hooked in the top of her underpants and he pulled them off, then ran his hand back up her leg, fingers stroking and exploring until she found herself groaning from the unbearable tension. Her knees were shaking as he parted her legs. She thought she had run the gamut of prolonged pleasure until he knelt over her and began kissing her legs, beginning at the ankles and working his way up. She was writhing wildly by the time he reached her thighs, and she could feel his shaky breath against the sensitive skin there.

He slid his body over hers then, the wiry hair on his chest rubbing against her already heated flesh, arousing her to a pinnacle of desire. She murmured his name, and their lips finally met as he answered her with a soul-searching kiss. He plundered her mouth until she was mindless, and then he took her in the mountain smoke with the sound of the wind whispering over them. Molly clutched him to her, wanting the pleasure and succor he offered so readily. Those changes deep inside her, those subtle changes that had begun in the trench in Sean's arms, were coming to fruition. Like the caterpillar in the cocoon, she was emerging from her self, reborn with wings. Locked in Sean's arms, she soared with him over the mountains on gossamer smoke, two lovers in the timeless moonlight.

And at the apex of the flight, Sean kissed her deeply, his body worshiping hers with its own erotic dance. In her heart Molly reached for the moon and caught it in her arms. Its brightness was dazzling to the senses, heating her soul to the very core. Light exploded inside her, engulfed her, and she and Sean spiraled upward into the night, up to the stars.

"I love you, Molly," he cried raggedly. He buried his head against her neck as their bodies shuddered with the power of tension unleashed. They clung to each other damply, their breath warm on each other's flesh, and the night embraced them. Sean pulled his jacket around her and covered her with his own warm body, and she immersed herself in all the sensations of Sean: the rough wool of his jacket prickling on her bare skin; the wiry tickling of his chest pressing her breasts; the scent of pine and salty perspiration that clung to his skin.

He pulled her shirt back around her, fastening the buttons crookedly, so that she had one button left over at the top and an empty buttonhole at the bottom. They were giggling like two schoolchildren as he pulled her panties and slacks back up, and then she rolled him over on his back, straddling him while she clumsily tried to dress him in turn. In the end he had to help her because they were both laughing so hard.

Arm in arm, they ran to her jeep. "I hope nothing important got frostbitten," he teased as he climbed in behind the wheel.

"Just my brain," she said ruefully, rubbing her hands together for warmth.

"Good," he said. "Nothing important. I love sexy, empty-headed women."

She punched him lightly on the arm, then settled back in her seat for the short ride home.

"You know," he said quietly as they drew up to the ranger station, "I have never in my life needed a woman so badly that I made love to her in the middle of a forest when shelter was just a few minutes away." He turned to Molly, his fingers brushing her shoulder. "And I've never so achingly needed that woman again just a few minutes later." The silvery moonlight turned his green eyes to that same shade again — the olivine crystal — and Molly found herself willingly falling back into their depths.

"Let's go in," she whispered. "You can show me how much we need each other by a fire."

Sean built the fire while Molly let Thoreau out of his cage and heated some soup on the stove; then he went to shower. Molly was humming and slicing French bread when she heard a loud thump in the bathroom, followed by a burst of surprised laughter. She dried her hands on her apron as she hurried to the bathroom. The door stood partway open, and when she poked her head in she saw Thoreau hunched indignantly on the bathroom counter, his paws gripping a pear. The sink had been drained, and Thoreau's whiskers were bristling.

Molly smiled, but the laughter caught in her throat when she saw Sean in the mirror. He stood wrapped in only a towel, his hair glistening with water from the shower, his skin warm and burnished and sweet-smelling. Molly swallowed as their eyes met in the mirror. "I've been leaving water in the sink for Thoreau," she explained hesitantly. "He likes to rinse his food off there. He even washes his granola bars. Makes a real mess."

Sean's only answer was to pull her into the room and into his damp arms. She fell against him while he rained kisses on her hair and neck, her hands clutching his shoulders. When he finally stood back she was breathless. "I'd better get dinner on," she murmured, "or they'll find us starved to death in each other's arms."

"I can think of worse ways to go," he said wickedly.

"Is that so?" she teased him, striking a seductive pose against the doorway. She ran for the kitchen, laughing as he managed to land a playful swipe on her bottom.

She washed the dishes after dinner, and he opened the drawer to get a dishtowel, holding up the lavender camisole with an amused lift of his eyebrows.

Belatedly she remembered shoving it into the drawer one morning after a night of frustrating dreams, all centering around

Sean. "At least I didn't burn it," she offered.

Nothing would do but for Sean to see her in it. So they wound up before the fire, Molly in the camisole and both of them wrapped in a blanket. "This is an old family tradition," Sean informed her seriously as he held the wire popcorn-popper over the flames with two of the chestnuts inside. "That big nut is mine and the little one is yours. The object is to cheer your chestnut to pop first."

"Why do I get the small chestnut?" she complained, leaning back against him.

"Because I'm bigger," he answered immediately.

"In all departments." She laughed, and Sean kissed her upturned face.

"Shut up and drink your wine," he growled. "And encourage your chestnut."

Molly's chestnut popped first, much to Sean's consternation and her delight, and they cozily continued the game wrapped in each other's arms. An hour later the wine bottle was nearly empty, the fire was burning low, and they had eaten most of the chestnuts. They were entwined in each other's arms in front of the fire and Sean was nibbling at the ribbons that barely held the camisole closed.

"I like these old family traditions," Molly

murmured a little tipsily. "But who in your family sat around in a camisole?"

"My great-aunt Lillian," he informed her immediately. "She was the family sex fiend."

"Obviously you've inherited her genes," Molly observed as Sean untied the first ribbon, a triumphant gleam in his eyes.

"Those and her penchant for roasted chestnuts," he admitted, easing away the next ribbon with his teeth. His mouth grazed the exposed flesh just above her breasts.

"I think I like your great-aunt Lillian," she murmured, drawing his head back to the ribbons. "And your family traditions." The fire sputtered down to embers as the last ribbon came undone.

"Are you happy?" Sean asked softly. She darted a look to his face, saw the last glow from the fireplace burnishing his cheekbones. And in his eyes concern for her. She couldn't remember anyone ever asking her that before, and it touched her.

"Yes," she whispered, letting the word linger on her tongue, savoring the circle of his arms. "More than happy. Whole. Belonging." She nuzzled her cheek against his shirt. "Remember the night you told me about the constellations and the planets and how they're spinning in space in precise orbits?"

"And we're voyagers on the planet Earth," he added with a gentle smile.

She nodded. "For once I feel like I'm part of the rhythm of the universe, a true voyager, not just a spectator."

She would have said more, but his mouth closed over hers just then, catching the last words and turning them into a sigh. She felt his warm breath against her lips as he raised his head slightly. "Sometimes you can't see the constellations," he murmured, "because the clouds block them out or it's the day and the sun's brightness outshines them. But they're always there, Molly, just like this bond between us, sometimes invisible but as real as the stars."

Stars. She felt free and light, as though she were traveling through space right now. It seemed she could go anywhere, do anything when Sean held her like this, safe in his arms.

Insistently Sean covered her mouth with his. He reached behind her to set her wineglass on the hearth and laid her backwards on the rug, his mouth still clinging to hers. Sean's kiss deepened, and the stars all swirled in Molly's head. The last chestnut popped in the wire basket, now forgotten by the fire, as Sean rolled over on top of her.

Chapter 9

Molly and Sean awoke in each other's arms the next morning, the blanket tangled around their legs. The fire was dead and the hearth cold to the touch. Laughing and stumbling over the blanket, they made their way to the kitchen and started the coffee. Molly poked a granola bar into the hollow log beside the couch, and a sleepy Thoreau blinked at her. "I feel like I should tune the TV in to Sesame Street for him," she remarked ruefully to Sean.

"That's all we need," he said. "A raccoon who knows how to read and write. He'll drive us crazy with his demands. First it's granola bars, then it'll be a bed, and soon a car of his own."

"And then a houseful of his teenage friends," Molly agreed.

"Where do you want to go today?" he asked, circling his arm around her waist and drawing her to him.

"I want to see your Freestone Foundation

exhibit," she said, "and then I'm taking you shopping."

Sean made a face. "Shopping?"

"A very special place. You'll like it."

"If you say so."

An hour later his arm was still around her waist, but they were walking down the main hall of the Freestone Foundation in town. Molly was wearing a sky-blue sweater that matched her eyes and a pair of powder-blue corduroy slacks. It had been a struggle getting dressed with Sean determined to take off her clothes as fast as she could put them on, but eventually she'd evaded him with lewd promises for tonight.

They paused in front of a display case filled with native mushrooms. Molly had run across each of them at one time or another, and she told Sean where they could be found — the fiery orange-peel fungus, the angel's wings and fairy-ring mushrooms.

The next case housed a rock collection, and Molly flushed slightly when she saw a piece of pyrite. "My three contributions," Sean said, pointing to the top row. "Pyrite, barite, and muscovite."

"Where's your olivine crystal?" she asked.

"They already had one." He pointed to the middle row. "And I kind of wanted to keep the one I found." His eyes turned smoky while she watched him, and Molly wondered what he was thinking. His hand tightened on her waist as he guided her to the next display. Molly's eyes brightened when she saw that the whole display case was filled with Sean's photographs of flowers, trees, and butterflies.

"There's a swallowtail," she exclaimed, "and a rhododendron and — good heavens, Sean! — that's Thoreau after the fire!" There he was, a little charred bundle, huddled by a tree, staring at the camera with drooping whiskers and wide eyes. "How he's changed," she mused.

"Children do grow up," Sean said dryly, and she gave him a quick look. That enigmatic haze was clouding his eyes again, and she felt as though the mountain smoke had rolled into this massive hall and woven a web between them. For a fleeting moment she could feel Sean slipping away from her, and it was as though an icy hand had touched her back.

"Come on," he said, rousing himself and smiling down at her "It's a beautiful day outside. Let's go enjoy it."

The click of their heels echoed on the tile floor, and Molly didn't shake that shivery feeling of separation until they stepped out into the sunshine. Then she took a deep breath, feasting her eyes on the bountiful fall leaves that were glowing in shades of wine and ripe cheese.

She directed him down a country road where the red and gold foliage almost met over the top of the truck, and Black Angus cattle stopped grazing to stare at them from fields turned amber. They passed barns with sheaves of dried brown tobacco poking out of the slats and farms with neat split-rail fences. She had him turn by a white clapboard church with a shiny bell in the cupola, and Sean cast her a sideways glance. "We're almost there," she promised.

"Strange place for a shopping excursion," he said doubtfully.

They rounded a bend, and Molly laughed at the look of surprise on Sean's face. It was an old farm, but the barn and surrounding grounds had been turned into a flea market with a gaggle of folding tables and crowds of leisurely Saturday shoppers.

Sean parked the truck by the fence and helped her climb down. "A friend of mine is an antiques dealer," she explained. "She told me about this place."

"You're full of surprises, you know that?" he said as he took her arm. They walked up the dirt road between the fences, and Molly felt her heart quicken from the pressure of Sean's hand and the possessive look in his eyes.

They wandered among the tables, fingering stuffed calico animals and soft country quilts. "Look!" Molly cried, pulling Sean toward a portable clothes rack. "This is always my favorite spot. The woman runs a used-clothing store in Hendersonville during the week." Molly extricated a shiny black cane with a gilt handle from an umbrella stand and held it out to him. The sun caught the metal and sent out piercing rays. "Are you feeling particularly gentlemanly today?" she asked with a sly smile.

Sean regarded the cane with one lifted brow. "Find me a top hat to go with it, and I might be interested," he replied. He stood watching her, his arms crossed over his chest, his eyes sending her powerful signals that had nothing to do with the flea market. With an engaging grin he turned to a rack and began going through the clothes. Molly smiled to herself and continued her own sartorial explorations. Five minutes later she held up a black wool cape triumphantly. "Now this is you," she declared emphatically, tugging on Sean's sleeve to disengage him from a pile of velvet and silk on a nearby table.

Sean straightened and regarded the cape critically. His eyes swung to Molly, and the glint there caused a shiver to run down her spine. Slowly his fingers took the cape from her, and he swung it around his shoulders. It swirled dramatically as a cool breeze wafted across the field, ruffling Sean's rich, tobacco-tinted hair and carrying Molly back to childhood fantasies. Sean was a vision from an old book of fables, and she remembered girlish daydreams in the forest when she imagined herself stepping into a picturebook. "You look very gallant," she murmured softly, her fingers idly stroking a silk scarf she'd picked up.

"Here, my sweet lady," he said lightly. "I've found something for you." He plucked a hat from the table and set it on her head, his hands toying with her hair as he did so. "Come here," he said, "and look at us." He led her to an enormous gilt-edged mirror with beveled edges that was hung on a tree by the cluster of tables.

As Molly stared into the mirror, she could hardly believe her eyes. The hat was black velvet, large-brimmed and decorated with purple ostrich feathers that swooped over the edge to tickle her cheek. She saw herself transformed. She was standing beside a handsome man in a cape, and she touched his arm to prove to herself that he was real and not a figment of her imagination. His hand immediately found her waist and curled her to his warmth. In the mirror Molly saw herself standing with her lover. The word rolled around her head like a blossom, flowering into intimate beauty. Sean was so real and so necessary to her just then that it hurt. Some of her vulnerability shone back at her through the pensive blue eyes in the mirror, and she saw Sean catch that look and immediately pull her even closer, one hand smoothing back a purple plume.

"Aren't we great together?" he whispered, his head bending down to hers.

She nodded, unable for the moment to make her voice work.

"What is it, honey?" he asked gently. "What's the matter?"

She shook her head slowly. "My grandmother had a mirror like that," she mused, half to herself. "I didn't even remember it until now." A brief scene came to mind: She and Sue were sitting on a big four-poster bed with a chenille spread, giggling as they draped their grandmother's jewelry around their necks. They admired themselves in a big gilt-edged mirror above the dresser. Then there was a phone call and . . .

"What is it?" Sean asked quietly, his hand gently coaxing her face around to him. His knuckle stroked her throat.

Her voice sounded odd to her own ears when she spoke. "I was remembering a day not long after my father died when Sue and I were at Gram's. We'd been staying there while Mom looked for work. We were playing in front of that mirror when a phone call came. Mom hadn't found anything, and an aunt was calling to say I could stay with her awhile. I remember sitting on the bed while Gram packed my things. I felt like I'd stepped through that mirror into a dream — a nightmare. Suddenly I was going somewhere alone, without Mom or Sue. Like I told you, Sean, it turned out that was just the first of many houses where I stayed."

"You never knew any stability at all, did you?" Sean asked quietly.

Molly shook her head. "That marked the last day of permanence in my life."

Sean regarded her with a piercing gaze that seemed both searching and tender. "Molly Carter," he whispered, "from now on I'm going to be a permanent fixture in your life. I promise." Sensual lips nuzzled her neck before he brushed her mouth, his hands cradling her head. "Would I be too forward, lovely lady," he whispered, "if I asked you to spend that life with me?"

He enfolded her in the cape with him, and she felt as though he'd enfolded her in a magical spell where time stood still. It was almost like going back through that mirror in her grandmother's room.

"I'm shocked, sir," she whispered back, feeling whimsical in her fairy-tale hat. It was pretend and yet it wasn't. What was it he'd just asked her? Spend her life with him . . . ? "And all along I thought your intentions were dishonorable."

"My intentions," he said, his eyes molten green crystal as he stared down at her, "are to love you so much that you'll never again feel that emotional hunger you grew up with. Never, Molly. And we'll shower our children with so much love that they'll grow up with the best possible memories."

Children. The warmth of the day slipped away from her as though the earth had made a quarter-turn in the last minute. The dream of a home with a husband like Sean and his children was so tantalizing that it made her heart pound, but she was afraid to reach for that dream. What if she got it all — and then lost it? She dragged her hands from Sean's chest and pressed them tightly together at her waist. "Maybe we ought to go now," she said distractedly, glancing around at the other shoppers who seemed oblivious of the man and woman before the gilt-edged mirror.

Sean's hands moved to her shoulders, holding her there in front of him. "What are you so afraid of, Molly?" he asked quietly. "Is it marriage or children or what?"

She stared back at him, wondering how to explain it all. To someone like Sean, her hesitation must seem foolish, and yet he was looking at her with gentle understanding.

"It's all of that, isn't it?" he said. "You're like the small child with a brightly colored balloon that bursts in your face. You want another one so badly, but you're terrified it will blow up too." He pulled her closer to him and pressed her against his chest, the ridiculous hat with its ostrich feathers crushed between them. "Honey, we'll make a wonderful family. And you'll make a terrific mother. You can't worry so much about losing something that you won't let yourself have it at all."

"Sean, you don't have the power to make everything all right," she said shakily. "And as wonderful as marriage and children might be, they don't solve everything."

"Of course not," he said forcefully, his fingers tightening where they held her to him. "But we have the power, Molly, you and I. Together we can do anything."

Her eyes closed heavily, and she shook her head. "You make it sound so simple. Just a matter of positive thinking."

His smile was rueful when she glanced at his face. "Honey, if it were just a matter of positive thinking, you and I would already be on our honeymoon and getting started on those children."

Molly flushed as she caught a woman shopper observing them curiously. "I must seem very cold to you," she murmured quickly.

Sean's laughter disabused her of that notion immediately. "You're one of the warmest women I've ever met," he said gently. "In fact, my dear, you're a hot-blooded little siren when you get me alone and you —"

"Sean!" she protested as heat suffused her face. She grabbed his hand and pulled him away from the older couple who had stopped to watch them.

"— let down that steel armor," he finished with a wicked grin at her, igniting that smoldering desire in the pit of her stomach.

Molly watched in bemused wonder as Sean convinced the woman at the cash register to sell him the gilt-edged mirror along with the cape and hat. The clerk, a wisp of white hair and tweed, smiled at them benignly as they walked to the truck in the hat and cape, Sean carrying the mirror. He loaded it in the back, wrapping it in a blanket, and climbed into the driver's seat next to Molly. One finger reached out to flick an ostrich feather. Smiling, he started the truck and turned the radio on.

Molly leaned back and listened to the soft classical music, giving herself over to the gentle stirrings inside her heart. The ostrich feathers stroked her cheek and lemon sunshine streamed through the window and warmed her face as the truck bounced along. She gazed at Sean's profile as he drove, his fingers curved gracefully around the steering wheel, and her blood heated to mulled wine.

She kept remembering the pink stuffed rabbit she'd dragged from house to house as a kid, the one thing an insecure little girl was sure wouldn't go away or change. But it had, of course. Alarmed by the growing number of strains and smudges on the toy, a well-meaning aunt had put it in the washer and the rabbit had all but disintegrated. Molly had cried all night. She had kept that shapeless piece of fluff until her wedding night.

"Have you ever failed at something?" she asked Sean suddenly. "Something important?"

Sean gave her a sharp sidelong glance and shifted his hands on the steering wheel. "I can recall a resounding flop or two," he said lightly.

"But not one that involved another person and his feelings," she guessed.

"You're thinking of your marriage, aren't you?"

She nodded.

"That wasn't your failure, Molly. Your husband mined the marriage with his foolish exploits. He was obviously a very insecure man, and you had nothing to do with that." His voice carried a current of cold anger beneath the surface.

"I can't help but wonder if I contributed to that insecurity," she said pensively. "Maybe if I'd tried harder to be what he wanted . . ."

Sean's voice was sharp. "You can't become something else, even for the one you love," he said, and she saw the hard line of his mouth. "Ultimately, we're each responsible for our own happiness. We can't depend on another person to fulfill our dreams. It's too much to ask of anybody."

"How many dreams come true anyway?" she murmured with a half-smile.

Sean gave her another meaningful glance. "Real life offers more than any dream," he said softly.

Molly smiled. How many dreams . . . ?

He'd said she wore steel armor, and he was right. But under that armor was a fragile bundle of dreams, and she believed that Sean knew exactly what they were. In her bewitched mood today, she was almost willing to believe he could make them all come true.

A thick, gray cloud floated out of the mountains ahead and drew a curtain over the sun. Fresh wind chased through the trees, and dried leaves skittered across the road. The rain's breath was heavy on the air as they pulled up to the ranger station, though the rain had not yet begun. Storms sprang up quickly and frequently in the mountains, coming and going like the sweep of a hand across the sky.

Molly and Sean made it inside with the mirror before the first drops began to splatter on the gravel road. Together they built a fire and set the mirror up against the wall. It looked as if it would rain all night, and they curled up before the fireplace after supper, holding each other silently.

She could hear the rain falling rhythmically on the roof when Sean pulled her to her feet and walked her to the bedroom, his arm around her waist, fingers stroking the soft flesh below her ribs.

He laid her hat on the table by the bed and

wrapped them both in his cape. In the darkness and warmth, her heartbeat quickened as his hand explored and aroused. She sucked in her breath sharply as the fire he summoned forth in her burst to life. Her blood sang with her need for Sean. *Touch me. Hold me. Love me.* He slowly peeled off her clothes and touched her everywhere with kisses like wine. No part of her body was left unmoved by his lovemaking. He satisfied her with every part of his being. His hands, his mouth, his eyes all gave her what she needed without her asking. He created new needs in her and then satisfied those.

He gave, and gave to her again as though possessed, softly urging her to lie still while his hands skimmed over her flesh like quicksilver. He was determined not to take from her, she thought dimly. This act of lovemaking was for her pleasure. It was a gift from an unselfish lover. His lips touched the softness of her breasts, the curve of her hips, the creaminess of her thighs. He moved inward toward the burning core of her passion, igniting a trail of fire with his lips. She whispered his name breathlessly, like the wind calling through the pines, and he answered with his body, with an urgency that matched her own. Their passion carried them to the heaven, and as a fireball exploded within her she felt like a star herself, set in a glittering constellation with her lover.

She fell asleep in Sean's arms, the cape still wrapped around them. In her dreams she was a butterfly, floating over the forest.

Molly woke slowly the next morning, hearing the aftermath of last night's storm in the soft drip from the trees outside. Sean's arm was curved around her waist, and he was curled up against her. She blinked her eyes open and looked at the hat on the table. Thoreau was sitting beside it, swatting at the ostrich feathers and jumping back when they tickled his whiskers. A husky laugh bubbled up from inside her, and she felt Sean's breath on her shoulder before his lips kissed her there.

"Good morning," she whispered, turning in his arms to face him. "I could stay like this forever."

Hazy with sleep, his eyes were the shade of mist-shrouded meadows. "Time to get up, darling," he said, a catch in his voice. "I want to show you some trees, and they're a two-hour drive from here."

Chapter 10

Molly drummed her fingers on the armrest in the truck, stealing another glance at Sean as he drove. They'd already been on the road an hour, and still Sean had refused to reveal anything about their destination, except to repeat that they were going to look at some trees. "I look at trees all day," she protested, and he kissed her quickly. "Not these trees," he insisted.

She was wearing brown wool slacks and a cream-colored blouse with a high lace collar, a cameo at her throat. Sean stopped the truck to fill it with gas and came back with two snack-cake packages. "Not much of a breakfast," he apologized, giving her one, "but I promise I'll give you a picnic feast when we get there."

"Get where?" she asked sweetly, biting into the coffee cake.

"Uh-uh," he said at once. "No fair trying to trick it out of me."

"Perhaps I could wheedle it out of you

some other way?" she suggested, her eyes gleaming.

Sean sighed deeply. "Well, you have an hour to try," he said happily. Grinning wolfishly, he brushed a crumb from her mouth with his finger.

The North Carolina landscape flattened as they headed east, the mountains sinking down in a graceful curtsy of green fields and burbling streams. They drove another full hour before Sean stopped the truck again, this time at a small clapboard store with a squeaky sign that swung on its moorings above the door: CORGI'S MARKET. "Come on Molly," Sean said, leaning across to open her door. "I want you to meet someone."

Molly tested the store's steps gingerly, half afraid they would collapse under her weight, not to mention Sean's. The steps protested but held. Inside, it was dark as a cave and redolent of wood and sawdust. An iron pot-bellied stove dominated the long room, a cluster of wooden chairs sitting empty around it. The floor was of bare wood, worn to a smoothness that obliter- ated even the grain. Curls of sawdust sat like dried noodles in the corners and against the counters.

Molly slowly looked around. The shelves lining the walls were packed with canned goods, sacks of flour, and fresh breads wrapped in wax paper. Stacks of calico-print bolts lay on a marble-topped table. A sweet, pungent smell assailed her as she walked beneath cloth-wrapped smoked hams hanging from a rafter.

Sean propelled her forward to a counter at the back of the store, and Molly blinked her eyes when a hinged door behind the counter banged open and a little man in an oversized butcher's apron suddenly appeared.

The little man beamed as he wiped his hands on the apron. Curly red hair crowned his head like a flaming bowl, matched in hue by a pair of bushy eyebrows. Round brown eyes glowed with pleasure. He looked like an ancient elf.

"Sean!" the elf cried in delight, extending his hand over the counter. "I was wondering when you'd be back."

"I want you to meet someone, Corgi," Sean said, shaking his hand. "This is Molly."

"I declare," Corgi said in a soft drawl, shifting his gaze to Molly and giving her a beatific smile. "So she's the one."

"The one?" Molly said, bewildered. She dared a glance at Sean and saw him grinning.

"I've known Sean since he was a little boy," Corgi said, coming around the counter. He opened a candy jar and offered it to Molly. Bemused, she helped herself to a peppermint stick. "I used to let him have his candy on credit." Corgi shifted his smile to Sean.

"Corgi was good friends with my great-aunt Lillian," Sean said, squeezing Molly's hand.

"A great lady," Corgi said fondly, taking a horehound drop from another jar and popping it into his mouth. "I took her to the forest . . . Lillian's Forest." A sad note had crept into his voice behind the smile, and Molly guessed that Sean's great-aunt had meant a lot to him.

"Lillian's Forest?" Molly gave Sean a helpless look.

Sean nodded. "It's been in the family for a century. It's mine now."

"The trees you're going to show me?" she guessed.

Corgi wagged a finger at her. "The Feyer men only take one woman to see the forest. *The* woman."

"Now don't scare her, Corgi," Sean said mildly.

Corgi shook his head. "I didn't tell Lillian either," he said. He grinned at Molly. "I'm an honorary Feyer, so they let me take Lillian to see the forest."

Molly nodded as if she actually understood what was under discussion here. As far as she could figure, it had something to do with a family forest and a woman. She didn't want to speculate any further. Her brain was already reeling.

"We'll be needing some food," Sean said. "One of your home-cured hams and a loaf of bread."

"I have a great pumpernickel I just baked this morning," Corgi hastened to interject. "Not even cool yet." He bustled toward the back room, while Molly wandered around the shop with Sean.

When they finally climbed back into the truck, they were carrying the ham and bread plus several pounds of the miscellaneous goodies Corgi had kept loading into their arms.

"Is he really related to you?" Molly asked when they were on the road again.

"Not by blood," Sean said. "He wanted to marry Lillian when he was a young man."

"Then he's your great-uncle?"

Sean shook his head, his eyes turning smoky. "Lillian was in love with another young man, but he was killed in World War One. Lillian never got over it."

"She wouldn't marry Corgi?" Somehow the thought made Molly sad.

Sean shook his head. "They kept company

until her death, but they never married. Corgi's the one who named the forest."

"How sad," said Molly, intrigued by the traditions and tales of Sean's family.

"Here we are," Sean said, turning the truck down a dirt road off the highway. He swept his hand toward the windshield. "Welcome to Lillian's Forest."

Molly looked around, startled. She'd been so intent on Sean's story that she hadn't even noticed where they were — in a forest. On either side of the road trees stretched as far as the eye could see. Scrubby pines, timber for the future.

Sean eyed the scene as though looking for something special, and when he found it he pulled the truck off the road onto a carpet of needles beside a split-rail fence. He got out the bags of food and heaved them over the fence before helping Molly climb over.

"Perfect place for a picnic," he said with a smile of satisfaction. He spread a blanket on the ground and began unloading the bags. Molly watched him perplexedly. Sean was such a total experience that he could be bewildering at times. First off, why hadn't he ever mentioned that he had a forest of his own? And secondly, why had he brought her here?

"Sean," she began hesitantly, and he

looked up from the blanket where he was blithely slicing the ham. Slowly he stood up and brushed back her hair with one hand. "Sean," she said again in a softer voice. "This forest. How big is it?"

"Almost two thousand acres," he said, watching her face.

"Two thou . . ." Her voice died away. "And all of it's yours?"

He nodded. "Well, almost all of it. Come here."

He took her hand and pulled her into the shelter of the trees. Away from the sun she felt a chill, and she hugged her arms around herself. Sean stopped before a pine and tapped its rough bark. "This tree is yours," he said.

"I beg your pardon."

She watched his eyes turn that olivine hue as he wordlessly led her around the tree. Stepping behind her, he locked one arm around her waist and with his other hand levered her chin until she was looking up. And there it was — MOLLY, in white paint at the top of the tree. She shook her head, at a loss for words. Finally the knot in her throat dissolved. "This is my tree?"

"Mmm-hmm. How do you like it?"

"It's beautiful." Exasperation threaded her voice. "Sean, what am I supposed to say? You take me for a two-hour mystery drive, introduce me to a positively charming little man, and then prepare a forest picnic and give me a tree. Sean —" She broke off helplessly when he tilted her head back and kissed her. Sean's forest had an enchantment that was brewing in her blood like a magic potion. And his kiss only made the spell more sweetly binding.

The pressure of his lips was an ever-changing experience, first soft and coaxing and then deep and demanding. She gave herself openly to the kiss, melting against him when the hand at her waist wandered upward to her breast. His warmth was pervading her body. The treetops came together high above them, blotting out the sun and sealing them into this leafy bower.

"Let's eat," he murmured against her lips, drawing her tighter to him. Slipping one arm around her shoulder, he led Molly back to the blanket and began serving her generous portions of the food. She looked at her plate heaped high with ham, cheeses, Corgi's homemade bread, sharp mustard, pickles, corn relish, and a slice of Corgi's own sweet-potato cake, and then she looked at Sean. The slanting rays of October's sun touched his head the way it would a tall tree, brushing a burnished glow onto his dark brown hair and tipping his thick eyelashes with silver.

Sean had heaped her plate with more than food. Ever since she'd first seen him walking out from the trees on the day of the fire, he had been constantly heaping her plate with life. She had never felt so alive or so in tune with another human being. He wasn't a dream or a figment of her imagination. He was simply Sean, her lover.

"Tell me about Lillian's Forest," she said softly.

The green eyes smiled at her, but there was a touch of sadness in their depths, or maybe it was just a trick of the sun.

"Corgi loved Lillian very much," Sean began. "My father once said he thought Corgi fell in love with Lillian the moment he saw her standing in front of the fireplace in our living room. I wasn't born then, but I can remember later holiday gatherings when I was a small boy. And I saw a special look on Corgi's face."

"Love at first sight," Molly murmured as if that phrase touched something inside her and brought it almost to the surface. "Do you believe in that, Sean?"

He didn't speak for a second, and she registered the slight alteration of his features, the burning embers that flared in his eyes. "I believed in it one afternoon when I walked into a forest clearing and saw a woman standing before me with a can of spray paint."

She swallowed, mesmerized by those eyes. "Yes," she said softly. "I believe in it, too."

"I think Lillian loved Corgi, too," Sean said softly, his eyes still on her face. "But she was caught up in the past, in the memory of the man she'd loved and lost. That love had never been tested. It was first love in all its innocence, and Lillian couldn't let go of it." He glanced down at his plate and idly piled some cheese and meat on a slice of bread. When he looked back at Molly, there was an odd look of regret on his face. "Corgi brought Lillian here to propose to her."

"And she turned him down," Molly finished quietly, her heart aching unaccountably.

Sean nodded. "But he never stopped loving her. He fell into the habit of referring to this as Lillian's Forest, and the name stuck. That's what we've called it ever since."

Sean reached out and brought Molly's chin up, searching her eyes. "For fifty years this is where the men in my family have come to propose to the women they love." Now she knew what Corgi had meant when he said, *So she's the one.* She tried to speak, but no words came. Without unlocking his gaze from hers, Sean reached into his pocket and held up something that caught the sun. He slipped it around her neck and fastened it in back, and only then did Molly look down. It was a gold necklace with a single pendant, an olivine crystal cut in the shape of a heart.

"Sean," she breathed shakily. "Your crystal. You cut it."

He shrugged. "I figured it wasn't doing anyone much good, sitting home gathering dust. It's beautiful the way it flashes against the blue of your eyes."

Molly felt the pendant press against her throat as Sean folded her into his arms. "This is our own private forest, Molly," he whispered. "We can do what we want here." His hands slid over her body, burning through the thin fabric of her blouse, his lips nuzzling aside the lace collar to incite further riot where her erratic pulse beat along the column of her neck. She clung to him fiercely, returning kiss for kiss, reveling in the feel of his muscles tightening beneath her hands, the hiss of his breath as her fingertips traced a sensuous pattern down his back. He pulled her down on top of him, his hands splayed in her hair. "Marry me,

Molly," he whispered hoarsely in her ear. "I love you."

She buried her face against his chest, her hand lovingly slipping inside his shirt to test his heartbeat. "Yes," she whispered into the softness of his shirt. Then she flung her head back and said it louder. "Yes." The breeze seemed to snatch her answer and carry it to the treetops, where it was whispered over and over among the pines. *Yes.*

His embrace was almost painful in its tightness, but she welcomed it. She welcomed Sean and love with no reservations. Under a sky so sharply blue that it looked like an ocean, they undressed one another, slowly and with loving care, covering each other with kisses and caresses where clothing had been. When they were done, Molly was wearing nothing but the glorious green crystal, which drew in the sun and exploded it back into dazzling fragments, just as Sean's eyes bathed her in dazzling bolts of love.

"God, you're beautiful," he groaned. Fiery eyes traveled over her naked flesh, and she felt them as she would her lover's hand. They fastened on the pendant, green on green, and then his mouth swooped down on hers. She felt his palm pressing the small

231

of her back as though to draw her so close to him that they would become one flesh. They lay side by side on the blanket, ham and cheese and bread pushed aside as though this was the main course of their picnic, two lovers feasting on each other.

She sat up, wanting to touch him the way he touched her, touch him deep inside where the heart hid. He must have sensed her hesitation, for he smiled up at her gently and took one of her hands and pressed it to his chest, stroking it down toward his stomach. She grew more bold in her explorations, encouraged by the ragged sigh that escaped him.

Molly discovered a whole new dimension to pleasure as she moved her fingers over her lover's deliciously golden flesh. Each murmur from Sean, each sigh sent her own pulse rocketing in time with his. Giving pleasure was not a solitary act, as her pounding heart attested. Her hands played over his taut abdomen and lower, eliciting a low groan. He clasped her hands and pulled her down to him. "Enough," he breathed hoarsely.

She laughed, but the sound caught in her throat as his mouth closed over hers. Cushioned by the blanket, and the soft pine needles beneath, they lay entwined and let the brisk air nip at their naked bodies. Heat of their own making warmed them and fueled their desire. A few dried leaves rattled on the ground and raced away in the freshening breeze. They were oblivious of anything but each other as they made passionate love under the pines.

Molly half dozed on the ride back to the mountains, lulled into satiation by the afternoon of picnicking and lovemaking. She fingered the pendant, her head resting on Sean's shoulder, and listened to him talk about his forest. It was a good timber producer, and with sound management it would provide an excellent income. She drifted off to sleep imagining the two of them living there at the edge of his forest, together all the time, making love, growing old together . . .

Work in the forest took on a new aura Monday, and Molly found herself grinning foolishly all day long. Leif looked rather puzzled when he told her that one of the logging trucks was stuck in a deep rut off the road's shoulder and she simply nodded and laughed. She felt as if she could deal with anything at this point — stuck trucks, tree fungus, pouring rain.

Sean ate lunch with her that day and every other day of the week, and their eyes glittered conspiratorially as they contrived to hide their preoccupation with each other.

"Don't know what's the cause of all this joviality," Leif grumbled on Friday, his heavy brows knit together like a pair of mating caterpillars. "Damn rain's slowing us down to a turtle crawl, and you two sit there grinning like Cheshire cats. Don't make sense." He stared at them as if trying to divine the secret of inner peace and then gave up, shrugging his shoulders and walking away. A smiling Molly ducked her head against Sean's shoulder, and he ruffled her hair.

They had spent every evening at the ranger station, reading together in front of the fire, drinking wine, laughing. And most of all, loving. On Friday night, however, they decided to go to his house, and Molly took a deep breath before walking through the front door ahead of him. The house was somewhat unsettling, like a snag in the fabric of her security, and she didn't know why. All the warm, loving feelings she had for Sean were still intact, but when he flicked on the light switch, bathing the room in a peachy glow, those feelings lost some of their life, as if they'd been touched by a chill wind.

She covered her discomfort by heading for the island kitchen, where she busied herself preparing a salad. Sean came back from the balcony bedroom where he'd taken her small suitcase, and put his arms around her from behind. "Mmm," she murmured, laying her head back against his chest. "I hope Gil remembers to give Thoreau a granola bar, or he'll tear up the kitchen looking for one."

Sean lowered his head to her hair and she felt his smile. "You sound like a worried mother leaving her baby for the first time."

Molly smiled ruefully. "Just wait till he starts school. I'll be a basket case."

His fingers tightened at her waist, sending shivers of incipient longing down her legs. "Maybe he'll have a little brother or sister at home by then."

Talking about babies with Sean — actually talking about having Sean's babies — suddenly scared the hell out of her, and she cleared her throat nervously. "I'll have to chop up a few more hollow logs for the nursery," she said lightly, moving out of his embrace to pull some radishes from the refrigerator. She turned to face him, a small smile firmly locked in place, and found him watching her with hands on hips and chin tilted up questioningly. When she turned back to the counter and wordlessly began tearing lettuce into bowls, he opened a cupboard behind her. A minute later he was peeling potatoes in the sink, his eyes smoky with some emotion she didn't fully comprehend, but which chilled her already cold blood.

She glanced at him sideways, saw his hands working the knife quickly and efficiently as he cut the potatoes into chunks, the same way he chopped trees in the forest. His red plaid flannel shirt was rolled up to the elbows, and his jeans were coated with flecks of sawdust. His profile in the creamy glow of the kitchen light conveyed a tensile strength. The thought came to Molly with piercing swiftness that she loved him beyond all reason. She felt a sudden chill at the unasked-for warning from her wary subconscious that he might not always be hers. For some reason, she couldn't shake this despondent mood tonight.

"You know," he began quietly, his hands still working, "my family always considered themselves blessed with the best things in life. I can remember my father telling me that life was not a thing to waste on trivialities like greed or fear." He tossed the potato pieces into a pan and put it in the oven. Leaning back against the counter, he crossed his arms and stared down at the floor. He always seemed to understand her feelings. She didn't want to be touched right now, but she needed reassurance and she knew he was doing his best to give her that.

"I know what you're trying to say," she said quietly, her hands idly mixing the salad though her eyes were fixed on the stars outside the living-room windows: "Don't dwell on the past."

"Not just that," Sean said, shaking his head and glancing over at her. "A lot of people live in the present and still don't really live. My father told me that I owed a debt because I had more than most. That's one reason I became a fire pilot."

Molly clenched her hands, staring down at the sink. She didn't want to hear about Sean and his death-defying flights. She wanted to hear about Lillian's Forest and their safe life there. Sean could change, she told herself. He could learn to love the forest from the ground as much as from the air.

"Molly," he said softly, drawing her eyes to his own like a magnet. "Flying can bring joy to life. It doesn't have to be an instrument of destruction. I'm not out to cut my life short. I don't take any unnecessary risks."

She saw that he desperately wanted her to understand, and she did — at least in the abstract. To Sean, flying was simply an expression of living life to the fullest. And she could accept it as long as they weren't talking about hard realities. When he was with her, she sensed that he was still living life to the fullest, and he made her feel that way too. But they couldn't be together every minute of the day, and it was the separations that made her heart harden. To lose him someday . . .

He shifted his weight to one foot. "Loving is like that too, Molly. Caring for someone else can be the biggest risk in the world, but the rewards . . . Well, the price is nothing compared to the rewards."

She gave him a sparing smile. "I know all about those rewards. But don't tell me commitment isn't a high price. At least in my book it is." She caught the sharp look in his eyes and added softly, "I'm paying that price, Sean."

"I know, honey." He moved at last and enfolded her in his arms, and this time she desperately needed his touch. She clung to him like a dying woman to a lifeline, wishing things were easy. She loved Sean and he loved her. What could be simpler? Wryly she smiled against his chest.

Molly was restless all evening and only played with the glass of wine he poured her, swirling it in her hand and watching the golden bubbles rise to the surface. He sat beside her on the couch, his arm draped over her shoulder, his head back as they listened to soft piano music on his stereo. His fingers moved slowly over her arm, tracing a pattern, but she couldn't relax under his touch tonight, and she kept shifting her legs to another position, finally drawing them up under her.

More than once she glanced sideways at Sean and found his pensive gaze fixed on her face. She pretended to take a swallow of wine and turned another page of the magazine on her lap, but she hadn't read a single word in the last hour.

"Well, are we compatible?" Sean asked, nodding toward the page.

Molly didn't understand at first, but then she glanced down at the page and saw the headline: *"Lovestyle — Compare His with Yours."* She realized that the article she'd been pretending to read was a questionnaire on sexual compatibility. "I don't think we need a multiple-choice test to draw our own conclusions," she said with a smile.

Sean's finger moved up her neck to stroke the pulse-beat there. His smile was beguiling. "Besides, Henry David Thoreau wouldn't have approved of such stuff," he whispered.

He leaned closer, and she closed her eyes as he nuzzled her ear, his lips teasing the lobe to a shiver of sensitive awareness. "Let's go to bed," he murmured. "I have this multiple-choice test I'd like to discuss with you."

He could always make her smile. She leaned her head on his shoulder and curved her arms around his neck, allowing him to pull them both to their feet. She leaned against him, sighing into his neck as he maneuvered her toward the stairs. Everything slipped away when he held her like this — doubt, fear, the rest of the world. His arms were a safe haven he offered without reserve.

It was much later when she woke up in his bed, her heart pounding from the dream. Sean was sleeping next to her, and she watched his face until her racing pulse gradually slowed to normal. Moonlight spilled through the window into the loft bedroom, bathing her lover in silvery light. The sheet and blanket rode just above his waist, and his bare chest rose and fell with the even cadence of his breathing.

She slid out of bed and slipped into his blue terry robe. The sleeves fell well below her fingertips, and she pushed them up as she walked to the window. The night was perfectly still, and the moon and stars were reflected like jewels in the lake below. It looked so cold that she shivered. She couldn't seem to stop shivering then, and she hugged her arms tightly to herself.

She heard a soft creak of the bed, but before she could turn he was behind her, his arms coming around and pulling her tightly to his naked form. "What is it, honey?" he asked softly.

"I had a bad dream," she murmured, grateful for his warmth and comfort.

"Tell me about it."

"I was lost. I was alone in a strange city, and I didn't have a home. It was getting dark, and I couldn't find anyone I knew. I kept going from doorway to doorway, but no one would answer." She shuddered. "It was awful."

He murmured soft words of reassurance as he pulled her closer to him, his hands covering her own at her waist. "It's all right now," he whispered.

She leaned her head back against his chest and shivered again involuntarily. She pressed her eyes closed on a sharply drawn intake of breath. "Sometimes I feel so lost . . ." She felt his arms tighten around her.

"It's natural after all you've been through." His husky voice was a caress.

"I don't want to lose you, Sean," she whispered fiercely. "And I'm terrified I will."

She felt him shake his head against her hair. "Don't be scared, Molly. I'll always be here for you. You haven't had a home in a long time, honey, but you have one now. You'll get used to it. The fear will go away in time."

Home. She'd had so many homes and yet she'd had none. What was home to her now? There was only one answer tonight — it was here in Sean's arms. She turned in his embrace and blindly sought his mouth with hers. His kiss blotted out the bad dream and the night chill. Sean scooped her up and carried her back to bed, cradling her against his warm body and stroking her hair. He whispered love words to her, and she gratefully accepted all the tenderness he offered.

Chapter 11

They stopped off at the ranger station the next day, so Molly could check on Thoreau. Gil was just stepping off the porch toward his jeep, and he waved when he saw them. "Mr. Connelson was here," he called to Molly before he swung into the seat. "He left a note for you on the table. And Thoreau's fine. He ate like a pig."

Molly thanked Gil and hurried toward the door of the station. Connelson again. Had the Asheville position fallen through? There was always hope, she thought grimly.

Not only was the position still available, according to the note, but Molly's appointment had already gone through, and she was to assume her new duties in exactly two months. During the remainder of her time here, she'd be expected to wrap up her paperwork . . . She crumpled the note and tossed it into the wastebasket as Sean entered the kitchen.

"Looks like Thoreau behaved himself for

a change. It helps to keep him in the cage . . . Everything okay, honey?" She saw the tension in his face and the effort he made to hide it.

She waved her hand in the air, heading off his obvious curiosity about the note. "Everything's fine. Let's go back to your house now." She didn't feel like hanging around the station anymore.

On the silent ride back to Sean's, she gripped the armrest tensely. Dammit, Molly, a voice within her cried, why can't you tell him what's wrong? Sean will stick around during the bad times. Trust him. But Molly couldn't bring herself to speak.

Sean's face was grim as he followed her to his door. Molly immediately headed for the bedroom, ostensibly to freshen up, but in reality she needed to collect herself.

She didn't hear his footsteps on the stairs. But suddenly he was there, the way he had once stepped out of the forest, like a mirage. He didn't touch her, just stood in the doorway, leaning against the side, his arms crossed. The hard edge to his voice chipped at her control. "Out with it, Molly. What was in that note?"

She turned from the dresser where she'd been absently brushing her hair before the mirror. "It was just a reminder about the

Asheville job," she said wearily, suddenly wishing she could lie down and sleep for about a hundred years.

"A reminder?" His voice was sharp. "What kind of reminder?"

Molly shrugged as if it didn't really matter. "The job is ready whenever I am."

"Is that all?" he scoffed, crossing the room quickly to grasp her shoulders. He stared down into her face, his brow furrowed. "That's not worth worrying about." His hand left her shoulder to skim her cheek, coming to rest below her chin. "What's the problem?" he asked softly, turnding her face up to his.

She smiled ruefully. "You're wonderful at rolling over problems as if they're just so many annoying potholes in the road," she said unhappily. "But the problem in this case happens to be my life. My work."

Sean lifted his brows in a careless gesture. "We have Lillian's Forest," he said. "A forest needs a forester. And you're the prime candidate for the job. It would seem that solves your problem."

"Does it?" It was a question she'd been asking herself since they'd driven back from Lillian's Forest. She couldn't quite define the tiny snag in the fabric of her heart. Could she really quit her job and go to work for Sean? Put all her eggs in one basket, so to speak? She felt uneasy at the thought of committing herself so fully to him. Some small part of her couldn't quite make that commitment, and even a small part was significant. What was wrong with her? She loved him. She needed his tenderness, his passion, his deep caring. And yet she still couldn't allow her innermost self to believe that she and Sean were forever, that she would never again have to seek that indefinable haven she called home . . .

The gold flecks in his eyes glittered as he watched her. Such expressive eyes, she thought. They could make her think of warm meadows or stormy seas. He could be so many different things to her, all challenging, all exciting. There were as many facets to him as to the pyrite he'd given her, but Sean was real gold, right through to his soul. He was rock and she a butterfly in her chrysalis.

His hand caught in her hair and held her still as his lips descended to claim hers. No matter what happened between them there would always be this, she thought desperately, this need that was so consuming it had a life of its own. She couldn't help loving Sean on every level: physical, sensual, intellectual, emotional. Her lashes drifted closed on dazed blue eyes, beguiled by the spell of his touch. "Molly," he breathed as his mouth dropped to nip at the column of her neck. In his voice she heard the same iron core of love that ran through her own being. She fumbled to open the buttons of his shirt, her fingers shaky with the force of sudden emotional heat. He was a summer storm, claiming her with such abandon that she could only respond in like manner.

She pushed aside his open shirt and pressed her mouth greedily to his chest, her tongue tormenting his sensitive skin with urgent circles that moved concentrically to the nipple. She knew what he was feeling as flesh tightened beneath her touch. He had done this to her a hundred times, in her bed and in her dreams.

She felt his muscles clench as her hand roved over his stomach. "Where did you learn to drive me crazy like this?" he groaned.

"From you," she breathed.

"You're a good student," he said admiringly, his breath hissing out when her hand dipped lower.

He lifted her face to his and impaled her with his eyes. "I want you," he whispered. "I want you over and over, day after day, night after night. I want you with me all the time."

"And I want you," she echoed.

"For all time," he said hoarsely. "Not for a few weeks or a few years. This is forever, Molly." He pulled her tightly to him, so tightly she could feel his heart thudding against his ribs. He maneuvered her backwards to the bed and lowered her slowly to the soft satin spread. He bent over her, his face flushed with passion, his eyes glittering.

"Tell me about Lillian's Forest again," she whispered softly, wanting him to tell her that their forest was forever too. What she needed was some concrete reassurance that her future with Sean lay there. Forests were places that had come to mean security to Molly. "Was it always yours or did you inherit it?"

"It was always in the family. Some early Feyer settler owned it, and it passed through the generations." His lips brushed the line of her jaw. "Times were tough a couple of years ago, and my uncle was head of our timber company. He sold the forest to provide working capital for the company."

"Sold it?" A chill alarm ran through her.

Sean raised his head to look into her face. "I hated the thought that it was gone. It was part of the family, of our tradition." He leaned on one elbow and brushed her hair from her face. "So I bought it back."

"When?"

His eyes met hers. "A few days before I took you there. The day I signed the papers, I painted your name on that tree."

"Sean." Her voice was agonized. "You must have paid a fortune."

"Shh," he soothed, his mouth trailing down her neck. "The money doesn't matter. We have each other, and now I can give you a forest for your work."

She shook her head slowly in wonder. If he cared this much, then maybe she *could* quit the Forest Service. Maybe . . . "Sean Feyer, you never stop surprising me. You bought that forest because of me."

He smiled in unrepentant confession. "I'd have grown one from seed if I thought it would help."

She curved her hand around the back of his head and pulled him down to her again, savoring the taste of his lips as her tongue boldly pressed its way past his teeth. He groaned and met her rising passion with a kiss that rocked her with a swelling tide of desire. She was wearing a soft gray wool sweater, and Sean pushed it up impatiently, exposing a creamy expanse of midriff and the soft swell of even paler breasts.

His mouth lowered and tongued the flesh with soft, lapping strokes that left Molly shaking inside. Swirls of heat permeated her body as he created moist pleasure with his tongue, finally touching each budding nipple until she arched against him. Primitive, wild, abandoned. Her flesh was tingling with the physical and emotional maelstrom he had stirred up inside her. Her voice rasped when she said his name, and her hand raked his back possessively. She pushed at his shirt until Sean shrugged it off. And then his bare flesh against hers was so sweet that she groaned. She clutched his shoulders and felt the corded muscles tighten under her fingers as he brought his mouth down to the hollow of her throat.

She was drifting on a sea of sensual awareness, and she felt herself turning inward to that remote core of her being that burned with such astonishing heat. She was rediscovering herself in his arms, each touch he lavished on her awakening Molly to some new facet of her desire. And it was with delight and love that she watched the deepening green of his eyes as she stroked her hand between his thighs.

She heard the shrill ring of a telephone, but it was a long time before she marshalled enough rational brain cells to realize what it was. Sean, however, was glaring at the phone as though it were some rodent that had just gnawed its odious way through a wall. "Probably a storm-window salesman," he muttered, returning his mouth to her aching flesh. "They'll call back."

"It could be important," she said hesitantly.

With a low growl that vaguely resembled a hello, Sean picked up the receiver and held it against his ear in a tight fist. "This had better be important," he muttered.

She heard a voice of indeterminate gender on the other end, but the words were only a low hum. A reluctant smile touched Sean's mouth. "Yeah, you did kind of interrupt something," he said. His eyes swung back to Molly, and the longing in them made her breath catch.

Sean put the phone between his shoulder and ear and used his free hands to continue the loveplay over her body, his palm sliding down past the waistband of her corduroy slacks. Her breathing was ragged. She placed one hand against his chest and he caught it and dragged it to his lips, kissing it absently as he half-listened to the phone. "Mmm," he murmured huskily, then, laughing into the phone, "No, that wasn't meant for you." He shifted the phone to his other ear and laughed again, and Molly suddenly felt self-conscious. She pulled her sweater down when he shifted his hand to the phone again.

"Really?" he said, a new note of interest in his voice. "No kidding? A Piper Cub?" A cold sense of isolation claimed her, and she moved farther away on the bed. "Sure. I'd love to see it. Which airport?"

Molly felt a sudden chill in the room. Airplanes. It seemed they always came between her and Sean in one form or another. Even when he was only talking about them, they had the power to carry him away from her.

"Right. See you there in about an hour." He hung up and turned to her with a smile. "That was Rod. One of the guys from our squad bought himself a little used airplane. Want to go see it with me?" He grinned at her. "After we finish what Rod interrupted."

The invitation took her by surprise, and she covered her unease by fumbling with her clothes, straightening her sweater and slacks as she sat up. "I really ought to get back to the station. I have a lot of things to do this weekend. And there were some reports I wanted to finish for Gil." She kept up a running chatter as she got to her feet, looking everywhere in the room but at Sean's face.

She jumped when he came up behind her and touched her hair while she was getting her purse from the dresser. "It's the airplane, isn't it?" he said gently.

She froze, staring into the mirror at the

image of him standing so close to her, his face an unreadable mask.

"Molly." The word wasn't a reproach, but it was so vested with weariness that she almost wished he'd spoken sharply instead.

"I'm sorry," she said, speaking to his reflection. "The phone call ruined the mood."

"It's not just the phone call," he said. "It's because the call was about an airplane. Molly, I walk around the topic like a soldier tiptoeing through a mine field. One mention of planes, and I watch that expression slip over your face like a veil." His hands closed on her shoulders, and she saw his eyes harden. "You withdraw into your shell. You're doing it now."

Slowly she turned, and his hands dropped. Molly forced her eyes to meet his. "I think I'd better go home now, Sean."

"Dammit, Molly, don't do this to us. Don't close yourself off. Please come with me."

She shook her head quickly. "Not today, Sean. Maybe some other time."

"Some other time," he repeated tonelessly. He seemed about to say something else, but then he apparently changed his mind. "I'll get your coat," he said, abruptly starting for the stairs. Molly realized she was holding her breath, and she exhaled slowly.

They might as well have been riding in different trucks on the way to the ranger station. The sunlight seemed powerless to warm her chilled flesh, a feat even the billowing air from the truck heater couldn't accomplish. Molly hugged her arms to herself. The worst part was knowing that she had thrown up this barrier between them, unable to stop herself, and now she couldn't seem to say the words that would remove it.

Silently he walked her to her door, then leaned against the doorjamb after he'd unlocked it and handed her the key. "What are the game rules, Molly?" he asked softly. "What will it take to keep you from running?"

She faced him, her hand clenched around the key. "No ultimatums, Sean. Please just let me have some space."

"What about the fact that we love each other? That we're going to be married?"

"This isn't a question of love. You know that."

"Do I?" His tone was ironic, and it sent a sharp stab of pain through her heart. "Maybe love just isn't enough, Molly. It doesn't seem to stop you from locking your emotions in the closet every time you're forced to face something painful."

"Please, Sean . . ." she began, but her

words died slowly, burning out on the green fire in his eyes.

"Maybe you don't even know what you're running from anymore," he said somberly. "You're still living in a world where marriage is a prison built by two strangers. No," he corrected himself in a flat voice. "You're *existing* in that world. What you're doing now can't really be called living."

His words stung, the more so because he was standing only inches away and not touching her. She needed the touch of his hands and lips as balm for her painfully bruised emotions. But he made no move toward her.

"Please try to understand," she began helplessly. "I need you, Sean, but I can't force myself to pretend that something like flying doesn't bother me. What I'm afraid of is risk."

"I do understand," he said quietly. "But I think you've mixed up your definitions. You say *risk*, but I think what you're really talking about is commitment." He took a long breath while she stood paralyzed, a chill breeze penetrating her coat. She watched him turn and walk to the truck, his shoulders taut and unyielding. When the engine started and the truck moved away, she had the uneasy feeling that he was fading into the forest like the mountain smoke.

During Sunday afternoon's card game Molly's mother gently accused her of a lack of attention, citing the previous play when Molly had trumped her own partner's ace. Molly denied the charge, but minutes later she brought in a bag to refill the candy dish and instead dumped the contents in the ashtray on top of Maxie's still smoldering pipe. Maxie's face registered dismay and disbelief as a malted milk ball hissed and melted on his prize meerschaum.

She threw Molly a look full of sympathy, and after a long pause Enid said, "How have things been going lately, Molly?"

"Not well," Molly said tersely.

She carried the ashtray to the kitchen to clean it and was sponging off Maxie's pipe when Enid appeared behind her, patting her back as she reached around to set a glass on the counter. "I like your friend Sean," Enid said quietly. "He's good for you, Molly. He has the same appetite for life that you have, the same wonderful enthusiasm." Enid smiled. "When you were very little, you could hardly wait for the next day to come. It made me feel young just being around you."

"I love him, Mom."

"I know you do, honey. But I also know something's bothering you."

Molly shook her head briefly. "I'm not even sure what it is. I love Sean and yet something scares me."

"Commitment?" her mother asked quietly. "Marriage can be frightening, especially after a bad experience."

"I know."

"Don't let that fear keep you from your happiness, Molly."

"Thanks, Mom." Molly squeezed her mother's hand and watched her retreating back as she left the kitchen. Enid Carter was a strong woman, but Molly knew the suffering she'd endured when she had to farm her daughters out to other homes like stray kittens. Still, Enid had Maxie now, and Molly knew that when they got home they would brew a pot of tea and rehash the card game and sit in front of the TV like any married couple. Like Lillian and Corgi?

No, those weren't Sean's terms; he wouldn't settle for just a piece of Molly. And if Sean left her life, then the magic would go with him.

Sue lingered a moment as Maxie and Enid made their way to the car. "You okay?" Sue asked, touching her sister's arm.

"Just early senility," Molly said lightly, and Sue smiled.

"Men have that effect on women," she said.

"Some men more than others." Molly twisted her mouth into a half-smile. "The downright impossible ones can complicate your life beyond belief."

"Sounds like love," Sue said sagely, waving vaguely in the direction of the car as Maxie honked the horn.

Molly grunted. "They want commitment. And then they take over your life."

"That's love all right." She squeezed Molly's arm. "Take care, honey. And do whatever's necessary to keep that guy. He's fourteen carat." As her sister ran down the steps toward the car, Molly absently fingered the pendant beneath her blouse. So if this was love, why wasn't Sean here with her now?

"Because we're both so darn hard-headed," she muttered to Thoreau as she closed the door against the outside chill. He came to the bars of his cage and, taking a hint, Molly let him out.

She brewed a pot of tea and built a fire in the fireplace, then sat down with one of the science-fiction books Sean had given her, but she couldn't concentrate. Sean's words

258

about commitment kept haunting her. Was she really putting a lock on her emotions every time the issue of commitment came up in her life? She closed the book and stood up, moving restlessly to poke the fire's embers.

She wasn't trying to escape commitment, she told herself as she stared broodingly at the fire. She wanted a solid future with Sean more than she'd ever wanted anything in her life. He was an extraordinary man, more compelling than anyone she'd ever conjured up in her dreams. But commitment meant a lifetime, a lifetime of sharing and working together.

And one small part of her that had been hurt so many times before warned that Sean's "forever" might not last her lifetime. Despite all his assurances and all his precautions, fate might snatch him away from her. She had a terrible vision of herself and the children Sean wanted, all of them as homeless as she had been as a child.

She couldn't remain in this limbo much longer — Sean had made that clear today. She'd have to make a decision. There was, on the one hand, life with Sean, a life that carried the risk of pain. On the other hand, there was life without Sean — and that alternative brought the certainty of pain.

She moved to the window and stared out, rubbing her temples to ward off an incipient headache. Mountain smoke drifted through the trees, silken webbing hung with dew. It wasn't raining, yet the air was heavy with moisture.

Separation always brought pain, whether the separation was voluntary or not. She still hurt from Steve's death, not just because of the loss, but because of the guilt. They had each hurt the other, and neither had had the chance to make it right. Unresolved anger had choked off her feelings like poison-sumac binding itself around a tree.

And, like a spring wind blowing away winter's cold hand, Sean had come out of the forest and touched her. Now Molly stared out at the trees, wishing he would come striding through the forest tonight and leave a bag of chestnuts at her door.

She didn't expect Sean to take notice of her the next morning when she arrived in the forest at daybreak, stepping out of her jeep and pausing by the clearing where he was backcutting a pine with his chainsaw. "Down the road," he called, stepping back out of the way. In the moment of perfect silence that followed the giant tree's crash to the clearing, Sean turned and saw Molly.

She couldn't move, riveted by his eyes, which held her there like bands of steel. Her muscles refused to obey her brain's command to do something, to move her legs. It came to her, over the pounding of her heart, that if her legs did move they would probably carry her straight to Sean.

Slowly he turned back to the tree and hefted his chainsaw to cut off the side branches. Every move wrenched at her heart. She wanted to approach him and wipe that blank emotionless look from his eyes, but she was afraid of what might replace it.

He didn't show up at lunch, and Molly halfheartedly munched on her sandwich while remembering an earlier lunch of ham, cheese, and Corgi's bread. Her peanut butter seemed tasteless, suddenly.

When she got home that night, she felt totally exhausted. She opened a can of soup, but she didn't feel like finishing it and left the bowl on the counter. Thoreau, released from his cage, clambered up to the counter and delicately sniffed the bowl, then began fishing through it for noodles. His hair had grown back almost to normal, and he had full use of his legs again. She would have to resettle him in the wild soon. For some reason that thought vaguely disturbed her.

Molly, who had never in her life been sentimental about animals, had grown inordinately fond of this furry little demon.

"Your free lunches are almost at an end," she informed him gently, her eyes softening as he came up with a noodle on one paw and gobbled it down. She carried her tea into the living room and wandered restlessly from window to fireplace and back. She set the tea on the end table and picked up the chunk of pyrite, hefting it lightly in her hand. Lost inside herself, she sat on the couch and just stared at the rock. In each glittering facet she saw some scene featuring herself and Sean: dancing under the moonlight, making love on a carpet of pine needles, laughing and arguing as the wind sighed above them. They clashed in many ways when they were together, but always they fought for the love and passion they forged in each other.

Wearily she carried the pyrite to her bedroom, but she didn't put it on the shelf with her other rocks. She lay down on top of her white comforter, drawing a blanket over her, and cradled the pyrite to her breast. Slowly she drifted off to sleep, and all the sweet memories of Sean intertwined in her dreams . . .

The luminous dial of her clock showed

5:00 A.M. when she opened her eyes again. She shifted stiffly. The pyrite was still clutched in her hand, and she set it on her bedside table and massaged her numb fingers. She heard a soft rustling and sat up to investigate. Thoreau was perched on her dresser, involved in a curious exploration of the hat she and Sean had bought at the flea market. The raccoon pulled one long ostrich feather down to inspect it and backed up nervously when it brushed his nose. Whiskers bristling, he advanced on it again as though engaged in some ridiculous contest with the feather.

Molly leaned back against her pillow and watched. Thoreau was becoming bolder with the feather, bending it down with intricate skill in those paws. He batted it away and sat up as it flew back in place. Caught up in his game, he pulled it toward the dresser again, and the feather snapped with a brittle sound. Thoreau backed up and stared at the limp plume lying half off the dresser. He gave it a light pat and it fell to the floor. He stared down as if waiting for it to fight back, then apparently gave up and trundled down the dresser and out the door.

Molly pushed back the blanket and set her bare feet on the thick rug. Grabbing a robe from her closet, she started for the bathroom, taking one last look at the feather on the floor. For some reason the sight brought a lump to her throat.

Molly got to the logging site early, before the sun had begun its long climb to top the mountain. Silver starlight kissed the frost-crusted pine needles. She wandered through the trees, using her flashlight to find her way until she came to the stream where she and Sean had seen the swallowtail butterflies. The predawn stillness was broken only by the rush of the waterfall. She stood there for almost half an hour until she could see a pink wash on the lip of the mountain. It was still dark, but her eyes had adjusted, and suddenly she saw a cocoon on a twig near the stream. Sleeping until spring. For the last few years she had been in a different kind of sleep, emotionally numb and wary of any intrusions into her safe cocoon.

She spun around when a twig snapped, her blood gathering itself to thud through her veins with the force of the waterfall. Sean was standing just outside the shadow of the trees, his dark outline perfectly motionless. He looked almost godlike, his raw-boned form the image of power beneath an insulated blue shirt and jeans, the legs cut short so they wouldn't catch on his spiked boots. She felt the magic whenever he was near. She saw his eyes shift to the sky, and she turned to watch the dawn break.

"Capricorn," came his voice, deep and husky, borne of the forest.

The constellation grew dimmer as a faint glow blossomed in the sky, relegating the stars to obscurity for the day. When she looked back at him, the soft gold of sunrise was gilding his face.

"Sean," she began hesitantly. Now was the time to tell him how she felt. She desperately wanted to work this out. She loved him. He seemed to relax slightly as though he was ready to hear what she had to say. The tension must have taken its toll on him. The hollows under his eyes were darker and his brief humorless smile looked haunted.

"Come here, Molly," he said softly, and it was what she had waited to hear.

She started toward him, but before she got there an engine rended the morning silence and headlights swung over them. Molly froze. A jeep stopped and a familiar figure waved. "Hey, Sean," Leif bellowed. "Mattingly's sick today. Help Joseph with the chokers."

Molly sighed inwardly. The chokers were short wire ropes that had to be fastened around the massive logs before they could be hauled in. The actual hauling was accomplished by an engine, but Sean would be busy all day running from log to log fastening chokers.

Sean waved at Leif and nodded. The jeep pulled away, and he turned back to Molly "We'll talk later," he said, with no trace of that hard anger she'd heard in his voice the night he'd left her at her door.

More jeeps wound their way up the logging road, and with a lingering glance at Molly, Sean turned and made his way toward them. For just an instant before he left, she saw the indecision and exhaustion in his eyes. Her heart went out to him. He must be sleeping as badly as she was.

They ate lunch at different times that day, and the brief glimpse she had of Sean as she and Leif rode in the jeep toward the scaling site was little consolation. His shirt was damp with perspiration as he bent over a huge log to fasten a choker. There was a weariness in his shoulders that was more than just physical. We'll make it right between us tonight, she promised him mentally. Tonight, love.

The night came quickly in the mountains, a gossamer twilight suddenly flooded by blackness. Lights winked on the logging machinery for some last-minute work before the men went home. Molly and Leif were standing with Gil while he measured the cut logs and made deductions for defects. The final measurement of marketable timber was entered on a tally sheet on his clipboard. Molly and Leif were going over the figures with him when a loaded timber truck pulled up and Sean and another logger hopped out. Sean's voice was low and clipped when he spoke to Molly. "There are some deep tracks in the road above our site. Looks like a logging truck went up there. No return tracks. Could be timber thieves."

"I'll radio the authorities," Molly said, heading for her jeep. She was back in two minutes. "They're on their way. I'm going up there to check it out." She spun on her heel, but Sean's hand caught her arm, halting her.

"You can't go up there alone," he said flatly.

Molly wrenched her arm free and faced him defiantly. "It's my responsibility," she said.

"You don't have any idea what you're walking into." His voice rose and his eyes turned to chips of green glass. "This isn't your very own private forest. You don't have to defend it with your life."

A beat of silence, and then she said, "It *is* my life. And it's my job." She backed up a step before she tore her eyes from his grim features and got into her jeep. She forced herself not to look back at him as she set off toward the logging road.

Molly slowed down when she reached the spot where Sean had been working. She cast her eye over the ground cover and trees on either side of the road, watching for a telltale sign that would reveal the truck's hiding place. Her headlights picked up a momentary glint of metal ahead, and she halted the jeep to check it out. There it was — a logging truck partially obscured by piles of cut brush. The camouflage was almost perfect. Molly slowly stepped out of the jeep, leaving her flashers on to alert the conservation officials who were on their way. There was no one around the truck, Molly saw as she moved her flashlight back and forth over the area. Footprints looked fresh though. Someone had been here not too long ago. With any luck, they would soon be returning to load their illegally cut timber. It was easier for timber thieves to do their work in the forest when legitimate loggers were in the area, when the sight of truck tracks and the sound of chainsaws were commonplace.

Molly kept watch from the jeep another twenty minutes before the lights from another truck swept over her from behind. She relaxed when she spotted the conservation department insignia on the side.

The two uniformed agents were middle-aged and friendly. They thanked Molly for the call, and she credited Sean with finding the tracks. They moved their truck up the road and out of sight, then settled down under cover of some brush to await the thieves. With the situation well in hand, Molly headed back toward the ranger station. There was no point in returning to the logging site. Everyone would be gone by now.

A thick, blanketing rain cloud was moving in over the mountains, obliterating the stars as if a dark hand were snuffing them out one by one. Haze boiled over the road and shrouded the trees. She rubbed her eyes wearily as she neared the ranger station.

A solitary light in the window greeted her, and Molly stiffened. She parked the jeep and sat in it a moment, trying to pull herself together.

Sean's truck was parked in front of the station.

Chapter 12

He had built a fire and was leaning against the mantel feeding tidbits of coffee cake to Thoreau, who was perched on his shoulder. The firelight flickered in his eyes when he glanced up, and Molly inhaled sharply. A low rumble of thunder echoed in the distance.

Molly closed the door slowly, and Sean stared back at the fire. He exhaled wearily. "It took every ounce of willpower I had not to chase you up that logging road." She knew it was the truth, just from the effort it took him to say it.

"I had to go, Sean. Don't you understand?" She crossed the room to turn on the lamp and laid her jacket over a chair.

"I understand. But I don't like it. You didn't have to go up there alone."

She ran her hand through her hair, and his eyes followed the ragged movement, then flickered back to the fire. "I've had to fight for the right to be taken seriously far too often to worry about taking risks," she said wearily.

"You always worry about the risks I take, Molly, but whether you acknowledge it or not, you take plenty of your own." He turned to face her, his hands jammed in his pockets. At another distant clap of thunder, Thoreau leaped to the nearby end table and skittered down to the floor, hastily lumbering toward his hollow log.

"It's a matter of degree," she said immediately. "This was part of my job."

"What makes it so right for you to go running off to confront an unknown number of possibly armed men by yourself, or to battle a fire with little more than an ax and your own wits, and so wrong for me to fly a plane to do work for which I'm extremely well trained and experienced? Answer me that, Molly." The line of his jaw was unyielding, the side of his face bathed in hot yellow light from the fire. Shadows flickered across his features.

This was the moment she and Sean had been moving toward, slowly and inexorably, from the moment they met. This was the crux on which everything hinged — her acceptance or rejection of Sean's way of life. How many risks was she willing to take for him? How high a price would she pay?

"I don't know," she said softly. "I honestly don't." *We have your forest, Sean. Can't we make it our life's work?* She couldn't seem to find the words to say that. There was something different about Sean tonight, something that frightened her.

His chin lifted slightly and the green eyes assessed her. Still, there was something more behind that grim expression on his face, but it was as unfathomable as the mountains when the smoke rolled in. There would be nothing but a thick swirling of gray everywhere, and then the smoke would lift and beyond it would loom an incredibly large scarlet-hued mountain that took the breath away. She feared that whatever Sean was hiding might be more insurmountable than any mountain. And she wasn't at all sure she was ready to hear it.

"Do you want some dinner?" Molly asked quickly, trying to diffuse that odd tension she sensed within him.

His eyes brushed over her, touching each intimate place inside where no one else had ever reached. No matter how inaccessible she might try to make herself, Sean would always have that power to bore through the thickest wall she could erect. "Maybe that's what we need," he said restlessly. "Dinner." But his tone belied the words. What he needed was something else, and Molly was suddenly afraid she couldn't give it to him.

Thunder rolled in closer, like a giant treading the mountain, his footsteps shaking the earth and rattling windows. A streak of lightning lit the sky from peak to peak. Molly dished up the stew and biscuits, leaving one biscuit dripping with butter and jelly on the counter for Thoreau, who had been solemnly watching the proceedings.

"I'll have to give him my recipe file when I set him loose," she said lightly, trying to alleviate the cloak of depression that seemed to be enveloping them. The circle of light from the kitchen lamp bathed them in a glow that was a poor substitute for warmth. They ate quietly. Sean seemed to have withdrawn inside himself to a place she wasn't yet ready to explore.

"That's a hazard of living," Sean finally observed, watching Thoreau clean butter from his whiskers. "Sometimes you have to let go and accept change."

Neither looked at the other, and Molly knew they weren't really talking about Thoreau.

The wind whipped up suddenly, flinging dried leaves against the window. Molly stared at the gathering darkness outside the window. "Dry storm," she said pensively. "Wind and lightning but no rain. A good way to start a forest fire."

"This is the season for them," Sean agreed quietly.

Neither was eating, and Molly stopped moving her spoon in circles through the stew. When she looked up she saw that Sean was just staring into his bowl, lightly tapping the spoon on the table. "Well," Molly said brightly, her voice ringing in the silence of the kitchen, "this isn't really one of my better meals, but then I've made worse." The last word hung on the air, sounding unnaturally loud.

"The stew's good," he said emotionlessly, and Molly wanted to scream. *Just show some feeling!* She would almost have welcomed his anger or hurt — anything but this reserve that chilled her more than the most violent shouting.

"The stew doesn't matter," she said briskly, pushing aside the bowl. For the first time since they sat down she saw a flicker of light in his eyes.

"No," he said quickly. "It doesn't matter. And neither does any of this." He jerked his head to indicate the room. "I don't care where we live, Molly. That's not important to me. And neither is Lillian's Forest, other than as a means to give you what you want." He shrugged. "What matters is us."

She couldn't dispute that. Yet, there was something else that mattered, much as she wished to deny it. "You aren't going to work in Lillian's Forest with me, are you?" she said hoarsely, breaching the shroud that was hanging between them.

He shook his head sadly. "Not yet, Molly," he said. "Not today and not tomorrow. Maybe in a year or two. But I can't give you any promises."

"You never did," she said shortly, standing up and carrying her bowl to the sink. "I've got to give you credit for that. You never lied to me."

"Molly." The word was a command, invested with all the pain she knew he was feeling for her. He was telling her to turn around and face him and face their future together, but she couldn't do it. Her hands gripped the edge of the sink even as she felt his fingers touch her hair.

There was a moment of perfect stillness, broken only by the lashing of wind on the windows, and then came a pounding on the front door. Molly broke away from Sean, hurried to the door, and swung it open. Gil stepped inside, shaking leaves from his hair and jacket. "What a wind!" he chortled, and Molly wondered at his good spirits. "Hi, Sean," he called over her shoulder, and

Molly glanced back to see Sean standing in the living-room doorway. "Great news, Molly," Gil said, grinning. "The conservation agents picked up two guys loading cut timber onto that truck. They said it was a good arrest. I heard them on the radio, calling it in."

"That's wonderful, Gil," Molly said, trying to summon up some enthusiasm. "It was really thanks to Sean. He saw the tracks."

"Hey, yeah," Gil said, stepping around her and grinning at Sean. "Congratulations are in order. I hear you got your doctor's release."

Molly spun around and found Sean's eyes fastened on her, his jaw muscles tightening visibly. "That's right," he said quietly. "Thank you, Gil."

"I know it must be a relief," Gil said, turning and walking back to the door. "To think you might never fly again after making it your life. Kind of tough. I guess you'll be glad to get back up in the air."

"Yes, very glad," Sean said, his voice sounding hollow. Molly couldn't stop looking at his face, feeling an ache so deep inside that she was sure nothing could ever salve the pain. Here was the precipice she'd sensed in their future. She felt as if she had just stepped off it.

"Well, I'd better get going," Gil said cheerily. He glanced from one to the other and said, "Is everything okay? You two look a little bleak."

"No," Molly said quickly. "Everything's fine. See you later, Gil."

He took one last look at them before pulling up his hood and stepping outside. Molly shut the door and leaned back against it, closing her eyes for a brief respite before facing Sean again. It had finally come down to this. Even as she had tried to envision their future together in Lillian's Forest, the two of them working side by side, something had warned her it was a false dream. She had been feeding an illusion.

"I didn't know how to tell you," he said from the doorway, and she was glad there was no apology in his voice. She couldn't have stood that.

"I suppose deep down I knew it was coming. It was just a matter of when."

Slowly she opened her eyes and let the force of his presence across the room hit her with all its evocative power. His hair, clean and shiny, always claimed the light for its own, and her fingers curled at her sides with the need to touch it. Green eyes glittering with a light that never failed to set her soul on fire; the flat curve of his stomach under the shirt, firm hips encased in jeans, the hardness of his chest against soft fabric; musk scent and warm wool — all these sensory images ran through her head in the same instant that lightning flashed outside and drew her toward Sean like a magnet. But she couldn't move. She thought of his muscled thighs pressed so close against her own, the heat his body generated, the demanding feel of his lips on her own, and still she couldn't move. One simple fact separated her from the man she loved — the stupid, simple, unimportant fact that he wanted to fly airplanes over flaming forests. The steel skein inside her was slowly unraveling, leaving shards of her heart scattered in its wake.

"It probably doesn't matter to you now," he said, his face hardening as he watched her reaction. "But I was going to move to Lillian's Forest with you. There's a demand for fire pilots there because of the private timber land. And then when I tired of flying I could work the forest with you."

Unless you got yourself killed first, her inner voice mocked. She just stood there, unable to do anything, as he crossed the room and stood in front of her. She knew Sean was asking her one last time to accept him the way he was, to work on building a life with him. And by not answering she gave him her answer. Mutely she stared up at him.

"Good night, Molly," he said quietly. She took one step to the side, and Sean opened the door. He may have said something else, or perhaps it was just the wind whispering over the pines, but it really didn't matter. He was gone.

She couldn't sleep anyway, so she started the jeep before sunrise the next morning and drove to the waterfall again. In the first light she saw the bush where the cocoon had been, but it was gone. The wind last night had broken dead wood and loose twigs off the bush, the cocoon along with them. *One less butterfly.*

She didn't turn around when another jeep came up the road, not even when its engine ground down to a whine as it slowed and stopped. A door slammed. She didn't turn around; she knew it was Sean.

"I hoped you'd be here," he said behind her, his voice as rich as the music of the water cascading over the smooth, flat rocks.

"What do you want, Sean?" she demanded softly. "More good-byes? Sorry. I'm fresh out."

"Then why did you come here to the waterfall?" he asked softly. "You still aren't ready for a final farewell. Isn't that true,

Molly?" His voice was taunting, and she swung around, gathering what fire was left in her heart and shooting it through her eyes.

"Let's cut it off cleanly," she said fiercely. "Like a big pine sliced through the middle by the saw. Let's let it thunder to the ground and lie still. Good-bye, Sean."

Why was her voice so plaintive? He walked toward her slowly, those olivine eyes holding her rooted to the spot. He moved with animal grace, his head high, the first sunlight glinting off his hair and face, turning his flesh to polished marble much as the moonlight had touched him that night they danced. She had an insane desire to ask him to take her in his arms again the way he had then. But her mouth refused to say the words.

Her lips were aching so fiercely that they wouldn't move. The sun was directly behind him as he stood in front of her, and she couldn't make out the expression on his face. All she saw was a dark silhouette, arms akimbo, legs spread in a challenging stance. For a fleeting moment she understood the futility of resisting him. He was as unstoppable as the sun. Try to prevent it from rising and setting and you'd end up incinerating your very being.

His finger touched her neck very gently, sliding down her throat with breathtaking slowness, a feather drifting on a breeze. He followed the path of the gold chain around her neck and she realized his intention too late. A swift jerk of his finger, and the green olivine pendant leaped up into view from beneath her blouse. His eyes dropped from hers briefly, taking in the pendant with the slight twist of a smile. "You're still wearing it," he said, a note of triumph in his voice. When he looked at her again, his eyes were glittering as brightly as the trinket in the morning sun. Her swift outtake of breath was stifled by the sudden pressure of his mouth on hers. She was too stunned to move at first, and then she raised her hands to push at his chest. His kiss deepened, tantalizing her first into compliance and then a rising tide of desire that met his own. Her mouth opened in a wordless gasp of pleasure when his tongue penetrated, seeking her own. *Yes.* She wanted him.

Her palms moved restlessly over his shirt, impatiently seeking entrance. She had two buttons undone when he finally lifted his mouth from hers. She tilted her head automatically, trying to hold him to her, her eyes burning with need. His hands closed over hers, stilling her fingers. "All out of good-byes?" he whispered softly.

The blood rushed to her face, burning her

throat and cheeks. Her lips were still love-swollen from the pressure of his kiss, and she couldn't quench the fire she knew was burning so brightly in her eyes.

Molly pushed hard against his chest and wrenched her hands from his. She stumbled away from him toward her jeep. He called her name, his voice filled with impatience and regret, but she didn't stop or look back. She clambered into the jeep and ground the engine to life. She caught a glimpse of him in the rearview mirror as she sped away. He was standing rigidly, his hands balled at his side, his chin high as though he were holding himself under tight control.

She slammed her fist against the steering wheel and drove up the logging road as though she were driving to the sun.

Somehow she got through the day. It was a major accomplishment. Sean always seemed to be just outside her range of vision. She would sense his presence and look up just in time to see his form disappearing into the forest or into a logging truck. She would catch a glimpse of the sun glinting off his hair or the flash of green eyes in an unsmiling bronze face. And then he would be gone again. She left at sunset without saying another word to him.

Chapter 13

Three weeks had passed since that last good-bye at the waterfall. Sean had gone back to the aerial firefighters the very next day, and the forest had suddenly seemed lonely without him. He hadn't made any attempt to contact her.

Molly had wearily finished up the timber contract work with Leif, roaming through the forest like a sleepwalker, only dimly aware of the noise of chainsaws and trucks around her. More than once she caught Gil or Leif watching her pensively.

Fire was a constant threat, and she was glad when the timber crew moved out of the forest. Lightning flashed across the mountains frequently, and she slept uneasily, waiting for a call announcing that smoke had been spotted. Everyone was on edge. She could hear it in the voices of the fire watchers when they checked in from their towers.

She had found an excuse each Sunday to

cancel her weekly bridge game, and she'd cut off her mother's obvious concern with the explanation that she was just too tired from work. It was half true. She was weary most of the time, but it wasn't necessarily because of work.

She was listlessly fixing dinner when Thoreau trundled through the kitchen carrying the chunk of pyrite Sean had given her. Lately the raccoon had taken a liking to the rock and kept it with him like a favorite security blanket. Now he deposited it on the floor with a heavy *thunk* and began climbing the drawer handles to reach the counter where Molly was stirring some mandarin orange sections into a carton of yogurt. She moved the yogurt out of his reach and set an apple before him.

Thoreau slid down the towel rack with the apple in his mouth and headed for the bathroom. Molly gave a little shake of her head and picked the pyrite up from the floor, carrying it to the table with her yogurt.

She ate automatically, with no real appetite, her eyes focused on the pyrite. It was a reminder that she no longer felt whole. Sean had taken a piece of her with him when he went away.

Gloomily she raised her eyes to the stack of papers on the table — the timber reports on the sale to Leif. As soon as she completed them, her work here would be done.

Molly pulled the papers over and picked up a pencil to make some notes. She wasn't hungry anyway, she thought as she pushed the yogurt aside. On top of the papers lay the letter she'd just received from Mart Connelson. Molly stared at it, not really seeing the neatly typed page. She had almost memorized the contents anyway. The new job could begin even earlier than anticipated. As soon as she finished here, she could move to Asheville. Mart had added that he'd even wangled a parking spot with her name on it. *A parking spot,* for heaven's sake! To Molly, that was the last straw.

She had been procrastinating these past three weeks. The paperwork should have been completed by now. Yet she couldn't make herself finish it. She didn't want to leave here and move to the city . . . *Then don't!* she told herself, pushing the papers aside. It wasn't going to work. She just wasn't the type to have a parking spot with her name on it.

Before she could change her mind, she looked up Mart Connelson's home phone number and dialed. She took a deep breath and plunged in determinedly: "Mr. Connelson, this is Molly Carter. I'm sorry to bother you at home, but I've made a decision, and I felt I should tell you right away." It was easier than she'd thought it would be. Connelson was sorry that she wasn't going to take the job, sorry to hear she'd be leaving the Forest Service. She would be heartily missed, he assured her, a hint of puzzlement in his voice. And when he asked what her plans were, Molly was momentarily stymied. "I think I'll take some time off before I decide what to do next," she said honestly. "But I'll stay on here as long as you need me."

She sat back after hanging up and watched Thoreau delicately nibbling on the apple as he perched atop the microwave. It dawned on her that she, Molly Carter, a pillar of predictability and conservatism, had just chucked the only job she'd ever had. For a brief moment she envisioned herself on a street corner with a tin cup, Thoreau dressed in a cap and jacket cavorting for coins from passersby. Melodramatic, Molly. Her imagination was tending toward the absurd.

A flash of lightning briefly illuminated the window, and Molly got up and stared outside. The distant mountain peaks glowed with silvery tips as the sky was slashed by another brilliant streak. Molly pressed her forehead to the glass and cupped her hands around her face. The forest seemed unusually dark and impenetrable tonight, and very lonely. She turned away and decided to go to bed early. She could start updating her résumé tomorrow.

Molly woke up to the sound of the phone ringing. She glanced at her bedside clock as she snatched at the receiver: 3:20 A.M. It must be trouble.

It was Tom in the watch tower on Stark Ridge. He had spotted an orange glow that came and went in the valley. "Is it flashing with any regularity?" Molly asked hopefully.

"No," Tom said. "It's no airplane light or anything like that. I'm afraid it's definitely a fire. We had some lightning strikes in that area just before midnight."

"Damn," Molly swore softly. "What's the reading?"

"It's pretty far from here. I can't get a good sighting. Azimuth is eighty-seven degrees. I don't know. It's probably fifteen miles or so from my tower."

Molly made some quick mental calculations. "The south side of Thorn Mountain?"

"Uh-huh. I'd say that's where it is. Want me to go check it out?"

Molly sighed. "No. I'd better have a look at it myself. I'll call you on the radio."

"Okay. Talk to you later."

Molly dressed quickly, not bothering to turn on a light. She pulled on her jacket and grabbed a two-way radio as she ran out the door. The ride to the fire sighting was long and tedious. She had to leave the timber road when she approached the ridge, and that slowed her down as she cautiously maneuvered the jeep through thick underbrush and grass, the headlights pale beacons in the dark.

She stopped and stood up on the seat, training her binoculars on the distant landscape. Slowly she turned an arc. There it was. A thin trickle of smoke rising from the valley floor. She sat back down quickly and headed for the fire. She drove as far as she could and then stopped the jeep at a dense stand of dog-hair thicket — young trees grown tightly together — and made her way through on foot. Progress was slow, and twice she had to stop to hack away the underbrush that impeded her path.

She stopped at the lip of a ledge and expelled her breath suddenly. She could see the flames in the valley just below her. They flared up and then died down, pulsing like a blowtorch turned on and off. The fire covered about a hundred feet in a straight line, feeding on the dry grass of the valley floor.

Molly looked around quickly. If only she could see better in the dark. It was hard to judge the terrain accurately. The fire would move slowly as long as the wind remained calm. But in a valley like this a sudden wind could create a terrible updraft, sending flames shooting up and out. If they encountered trees or brush or the thick carpet of pine needles on the forest floor, she would have a full-scale disaster on her hands.

She raced back to the jeep and radioed Tom. In clipped tones she instructed him to send firefighters, with bulldozers to the south face of the mountain to block the fire's path. The dozers would have to cut a fire lane along the line of trees. A logging company had harvested trees there last year, and Molly remembered that the slash — limbs, tree-tops, and other debris from logging — now covered the whole south face. Although slash provided valuable nutrients to the soil, it was also highly combustible fuel for a fire.

"Radio the hangar and send a spotter," she ordered Tom. "We need someone in the air to watch the fire's progress."

Carrying her hand-held radio and an ax, Molly made her way back to the valley, carefully lowering herself down the side of the ledge by digging her boots into cracks in the rock and holding on to protruding trees.

She reached the floor safely and ran toward the fire, stripping off her jacket as she went. She began beating at the flames with the jacket, stopping occasionally to clear some brush with her ax. She moved ahead of the fire and used her shovel to begin a fire lane there. She shoveled steadily, barely aware of the passage of time or of the increasing ache in her muscles as she worked without pause. She felt a prickling at the back of her neck as the breeze picked up, and she raised her head in alarm. If the wind began blowing . . .

She worked faster, but the breeze at her neck grew stronger, and Molly looked around to assess the potential danger. She swore when she saw an orange flame on the other side of her fire lane. Somehow the fire had crossed the path she'd dug. Either the quickening wind had blown a spark across, or else the flames had followed a dead root underground, sucking in enough air through the dirt to feed the embers.

The new flames were only a few yards from the first stand of underbrush, and just beyond that the slash began. A sudden gust of wind sent sparks flying, and Molly flicked at her face as two of them hit her cheeks, stinging like pinpricks.

She would have to move up to the slash and try to clear a lane on the other side. If the flames got there before she finished it . . . She didn't want to think about that possibility. She could be overtaken by the fire.

She was growing tired, but she had to keep going. It would be a while before the bulldozers could reach this area, and she had to do what she could to contain the fire. She could see clearly now in the orange glare from the flames, and she picked out another stand of dog-hair thicket among the slash. If a spark set that off, she wouldn't be able to stop the fire, because then it would travel through the treetops.

She ran toward the slash and began hacking at the young trees. When she had cut several down, she got her shovel and started the new fire lane. If she could just get it ten feet wide before the flames got that far, she'd have a good chance of containing them. She caught her foot in a protruding root as she moved across the slash, and a sharp pain shot through her ankle. Molly forced herself to ignore the throbbing and limped on, digging up the forest floor with her shovel. The flames were getting closer, and she could feel their heat at her back, could hear the crackling grow louder.

She turned and checked on the fire's progress. There was no time to extend the fire lane. It was almost ten feet wide and stretched fifty yards in length. She glanced at her watch. She had been working alone for almost two hours now.

She went to meet the fire head-on. She beat at the flames with her jacket, subduing them, then shoveled dirt into the embers. If she could just hold off the fire until the bulldozers arrived, keep it from traveling up the face of the mountain. Sparks flew off the grass and she kept brushing her arm over her face. Her jacket was so badly burned that it was becoming a useless scrap, and she finally discarded it, pounding the flames with her shovel.

She was bone weary and her ankle ached, but she kept going, moving down the line of flames, fighting back. Just when it seemed she had it under control, a gust of wind blew across the valley floor and the flames shot back to life. Molly could only watch helplessly as burning embers flew high into the air and drifted across her fire lane. "No, dammit," she muttered furiously. The sparks were so close to the remainder of the dog-hair thicket that she held her breath.

She knew with sudden certainty that she couldn't defeat this fire alone. She needed help. The wind was whipping the flames up too fast for her to beat them back.

As if in answer to her prayer, she heard the

low drone of a plane coming over the mountain. Molly stared up at the dark sky, lit only by the hellish light of the flames. Smoke obscured her view, but she picked out aircraft lights topping the peak. "Come on," she murmured. "Over here."

The plane circled above the valley, and Molly's radio crackled. The transmission from the pilot broke up, and Molly couldn't hear anything but static. She grabbed her radio from the ground and spoke into the mike. "This is Molly Carter on the ground. The wind is picking up and spreading the fire. Can you spot the bulldozers?"

"Molly." It was Sean's voice coming back to her on the radio, and she felt a pang of relief in the pit of her stomach. "Are you okay?"

"Yes, just tired."

"The dozers are working their way down from the other side of Thorn Mountain. They couldn't get past a drop-off from this side. They should be there in another half-hour."

"How does the fire look?"

"There's a flare-up on the other side of your fire lane, about twenty feet beyond that stand of pines. It's in the treetops. You'd better get out of there and wait for the dozers."

His voice was calm, but she heard the note of urgency there. Molly found a new supply of adrenaline surging through her. Sean was here.

The wind gusted again, and sparks flew over her head. Molly instinctively protected her face with her arm. A few sparks landed on her shirt, and she beat at them with her hands. She started down the fire lane to the left, limping as fast as she could. Overhead, she heard the plane circle and dip as Sean followed her. She was almost to the end of the lane when she saw a tiny spark land in a clump of brush. A split second later flames burst forth in her path. Molly spun around and started back, following the path of dirt she'd dug. Sean's plane made another pass, and she glanced up as she ran. He was flying low, trying to maneuver down under the smoke where he could see her. His voice came over the radio.

"You're headed toward a drop-off. Turn north."

"How bad is the flare-up there?" she asked quickly.

A second of silence. "It's traveling through the tops of those pines pretty fast. There's an opening to the right where the trees aren't too close together. Keep moving in the same direction, and I'll guide you."

Molly felt the hot wind at her back, and she glanced over her shoulder. The blaze, fanned by the quickening draft, had jumped her fire lane and was hard on her heels. She knew what an updraft in a valley like this could do to a plane, and she spoke into the radio as she ran. "Sean!" she cried. Her breathing was labored, and she coughed as she inhaled smoke. "You'd better get out of here yourself."

"No way, lady." His voice was bantering, but she heard the tension underlying it. "Start angling to your right. The opening's about a hundred yards ahead yet."

She heard the engine noise fade as he flew to the other end of the valley to make another pass over her. The smoke was getting thicker and blacker, and she had to keep flailing at the sparks that landed on her clothes and face. The sound of crackling wood became a roar, and in the next instant the wind briefly blew the smoke away and she saw the flames ahead. Good Lord! It looked like a solid wall of fire, and she was running straight for it. But Sean had said there was an opening, and she kept moving ahead, putting her life in his hands.

She trusted him. She had known for a long time that she loved him, but trust was a commodity Molly Carter had never given easily. It was one thing she'd always held back from Sean, and she knew her reserve had hurt him.

And yet he was here for her now, when she needed him most. Instinct told her he would always be there for her. He was the kind of man a woman could build a future with, a solid future with children.

She understood why he was above her in that plane, and she was grateful for his presence. They were both trying to protect something valuable, to keep the forest for the generations to come.

She heard the engine drone as the plane banked and flew back toward her. "Molly? I can't see you for the smoke."

She heard the anxiety in his voice and spoke into her radio to reassure him. "I see the opening!" she called. "It's straight ahead." There was a break in the scrubby pines, a spot free of slash and underbrush. The flames licked above the opening, leaving a tunnel of clear space below. Molly ducked between the trees and suddenly found herself on the other side of the blazing inferno. She halted momentarily and gasped into the mike, "I'm okay, Sean. I got through."

"Molly!" His voice was desperate. "I can't hear you. Are you all right?"

"I'm fine, Sean," she shouted into the

radio, then groaned as she checked the meter for the batteries. Damn. Her batteries had gone dead. She could receive but not transmit. She began running up the slope, trying to get clear of the smoke so he could see her. She heard the plane's engine grow louder, and as she looked up she saw him dipping low, flying under the smoke, just barely clearing the tops of the trees. Her heart nearly stopped. Frantically she waved her arms to signal she was safe. He was so low that she could see into the plane as it approached, and in the next second he passed over her and she caught a momentary glimpse of his face in the cabin. Lord, he was beautiful! She had never been so glad to see anyone in her life. Her pulse pounded with love for him. Her heart felt as if it would burst.

He had seen her! He wagged the wings and then pulled up in altitude. Her radio crackled on again as he transmitted, but it was a long moment before he said anything, and then she heard the tremor in his voice. "Honey, every firefighter with a radio is probably listening to this . . . but I've never been so glad to see your beautiful face as I was a second ago. Molly, I love you." His voice cracked, and the radio went silent. Molly dragged her arm across her eyes to clear away the gathering tears. "I love you too," she whispered hoarsely.

She could hear a motor approaching ahead of her, and she limped forward a few steps, waving her arms until the driver of the bulldozer saw her.

Molly stopped at a jeep farther up the mountain to take a quick swallow of water from a canteen. "Looks like you had quite a firefight on your hands," the young man said admiringly as he surveyed her. Molly glanced down and realized she resembled the damaged goods at a fire sale. Her shirt was torn and peppered with small holes where the sparks had burned through. She was more or less gray from head to toe, her skin and clothes soot-coated and caked with dirt. She pushed a damp strand of hair from her forehead and smiled at the man. "You could say that."

As she assumed control of the fire crew, she heard Sean on the radio again, giving directions to the first wave of bulldozers churning up a thirty-foot-wide dirt path in front of the fire. Molly took over on the ground and sent men fanning out on foot to find the hot spots still spewing sparks and flames, the dead trees harboring rotted wood that would smolder for days unless smothered. The noise of chainsaws split the air, a counterpoint to the snarling of the flames, and men cut apart the dead trunks, then moved back so the bulldozers could plow dirt over the red embers.

The fire was under control by the time Sean's plane turned back to the hangar, and Molly watched him leave, a deep sense of pride swelling inside her. They'd done it together. They'd beaten back the fire one more time.

She stayed on the mountain for another hour to make sure there were no more flare-ups and then caught a ride back to her jeep on one of the bulldozers. She suddenly realized that the sun had risen a long time ago. She glanced at her watch: it was almost 9 o'clock. She took a deep breath and started down the logging road, heading toward the ranger station. Mountain smoke had gathered near the uppermost peaks and floated down to settle like a ghostly veil over the deep green pines. The sunlight turned silver where it pierced the mist.

Molly felt light and free as the butterflies she and Sean had watched flitting over the waterfall. She wished she could just spread her wings and fly back to the station.

She pulled into the gravel driveway just as a truck roared up behind her, spewing gravel and dust. Sean leaped out of the truck a split second after it came to a stop, and she stepped out of her jeep and limped toward him. His face was a study in anxiety as she ran toward him, his eyes sweeping her from head to toe.

"My God, you're hurt," he cried, catching her to him and brushing back her hair in a shaky gesture.

Molly fell against Sean, and her senses reeled with the nearness of him. "I'm fine," she said, both laughing and crying at once. "For the first time in my life I'm fine."

His hands couldn't seem to stay still as they moved over her shoulders and down her back, then flew back to her face. "Nothing broken?" he asked worriedly, anxiety still creasing his brow. "Do you hurt anywhere?"

She couldn't seem to stop laughing, and he gently dabbed at the tears trickling down her smudged face. Slowly she sobered. "Is that position of chief forester in Lillian's Forest still open?" she whispered, clutching his jacket with trembling fingers.

"Are you sure?" he asked, searching her eyes.

"Yes," she breathed. "Very sure. Of us . . . and our future."

He pressed her to him, his lips brushing her hair. In a voice choked with emotion, he said, "Forever, Molly. Forever."

Chapter 14

Sean's arm was around Molly's waist as they stood in the shadow of a pine tree marked MOLLY in white paint at the top. Sean's fingers kept wandering up her ribs under her jacket, playing a sensuous rhythm just beneath her breasts, and Molly's breath caught in her throat.

"You shouldn't be walking around yet," Sean scolded her. "The doctor said to rest your ankle until the swelling goes down."

"I wanted to see the sunset in our forest," she whispered, her eyes shining. "And besides, I haven't walked anywhere. You keep carrying me around like I was a carton of eggs. My ankle doesn't even hurt."

"Arguments," he sighed. "That's all I get from you." He looked down with a cocked eyebrow as Thoreau sat up on his hind legs to tug on Sean's slacks. "That goes for you too," Sean said with a mock growl. "Now go find yourself a girl."

"Do you think he'll be okay here?" Molly

said, a trace of worry in her voice.

"Thoreau?" Sean said. "I figure that by daybreak he'll have found his way to Corgi's market."

Molly laughed and turned in his embrace to drape her arms around his neck. "Do you think we could get married right here?" she murmured. "Lillian's Forest is so perfect."

"I don't see why not," he said, kissing her nose. "And then we could honeymoon right over there under that tree." Smiling wickedly, he lowered his hands to stroke her bottom.

"Mmm," she sighed. "The honeymoon suite."

Sean leaned against the pine and pulled Molly to him. "Are you happy, love?"

"Euphoric," she murmured huskily.

"I want you so much," he said, his eyes shining with verdant brightness, a glow that matched the sunlight on the trees. He slowly lowered his head to nuzzle her throat, his mouth administering searing love nips that elicited a groan from her.

"You've got me," she whispered, clenching her hands against his shoulders. "Heart and soul, Sean. Forever," she said confidently. She knew the last ghosts from her past had been consumed by the fire they'd fought and beaten together.

Wildfire raced through her veins as Sean's hands went under her sweater, palms gliding upward to cup her warm, swelling breasts. His lips brushed urgently over her collarbone, and then he slid down the tree to the ground, pulling her with him, settling her in his lap. He pushed her sweater up and lowered his mouth to take one nipple between his lips.

"Forever hardly seems long enough for all the love I have to give you," he murmured huskily, his love-bright gaze lifting to sweep her face.

She fumbled with his jacket and shirt, fingers aching with the need to touch him, to feel his pulse quicken beneath her hands. His chest when she encountered it at last was hard and unyielding and matted with coarse hair. She curled herself to him, pressing her hand and mouth into his warm flesh, rewarded by the increased tempo of his heartbeat beneath her cheek.

The sun was setting beyond the trees, sinking like a red fireball. Dusk hovered over the treetops, a soft grayness that promised moonlight and constellations. The forest was settling into stillness broken only by the occasional soft crunch of a pine cone hitting the ground, the rustle of a bird nesting.

"Look, love," he whispered against her hair.

She looked over her shoulder and smiled. Thoreau stood at the edge of a clearing on his haunches, black nose raised to the air. Most of his hair had grown back by now, she suddenly realized. He looked quite . . . handsome. Then she smiled. On the other side of the clearing sat another raccoon, also testing the air. Thoreau sank down on all fours and began lumbering toward the other animal. Then he faded into the darkness, and the last Molly saw of him was a bushy tail twitching in the evening breeze.

She turned back to Sean, lifting her face with a smile. She didn't know a tear had escaped her eye until Sean gently kissed it away. It was a tear of happiness, and she welcomed the rush of emotion that overtook her as Sean wrapped her in his embrace. The flames of love coursed through her blood. She knew with certainty that she had a future and a home and love. She had her soul mate, Sean Feyer.

8-0/ DATE

GAYLORD No. 2333